# THE PRIN

Benedetto de Lyse can pick nearly any lock in the delta city of Ardent. As a common thief and lowly henchman of one of the city's shadow princes, his options to move up in the world are limited. Which makes his fascination with the charming Alessandra all the more tragic. She's a daughter of one of the merchant princes, and there's no way he'll ever be able to unlock her heart. Hell, she doesn't even know that he exists.

Yet when a rival organisation threatens to kidnap the princess, Ben can't sit idly by. After all, the Cordo family has a penchant for snipping off fingers if their demands are not met with alacrity.

In Ardent, caring about the wrong person can get you a slit throat and a pocket full of stones to drag you to the bottom of the river.

With time running out, Ben must act, even if his intervention threatens to spark a war that will rip out a city state's underbelly.

The Princess Job
Copyright © 2023 Nerine Dorman

First published by Ba en Ast Books 2023.

All rights reserved. No part of this book may be reproduced in any form by any electronic or mechanical means including photocopying, recording, or information storage and retrieval without permission in writing from the author.

This book is a work of fiction. Any resemblance to actual events, real persons living or dead, is entirely coincidental.


Cover Design by Nerine Dorman
Interior Design by Nerine Dorman
Proofreading by Cat Hellisen

This first paperback edition was printed by Amazon.

An e-book edition of this title is also available.

www.nerinedorman.blogspot.com

# THE PRINCESS JOB

NERINE DORMAN

# DEDICATION

*For Storm.*
*May Bast and Sekhmet*
*walk by your side*
*in the Field of Reeds.*

# CONTENTS

| | |
|---|---|
| Acknowledgements | i |
| Chapter 1 | 1 |
| Chapter 2 | 7 |
| Chapter 3 | 13 |
| Chapter 4 | 21 |
| Chapter 5 | 35 |
| Chapter 6 | 46 |
| Chapter 7 | 61 |
| Epilogue | 83 |
| About the Author | 88 |
| Other Books by Nerine Dorman | 89 |

# ACKNOWLEDGEMENTS

*I can never thank everyone who's accompanied me on the path of publication. My peeps at Skolion, Masha, Cat, Toby, Amy, Kim, Sonya, Laurie, and others, thank you. And of course, Helen, who watches the birds with me.
I couldn't do this without you.*

# CHAPTER 1

Her name is Alessandra Francesca Luciente. She is the most beautiful woman in all of Ardent, and she has absolutely no idea I exist.

Yes, yes, I know, some would say it's downright creepy watching her every Day of the Bells, when she visits the Isle of Doves Library, but truth be told, there is no lovelier sight in all of the Ardent River delta. At least by my estimation. Cael will disagree, but then I've told him numerous times that his taste in women is tawdry and predictable.

Ah, the lovely Alessandra. She is most deserving of my praises, for there is none like her in all the city, perhaps even the entire region. From her mother's side, it is said, she has inherited her warm, coppery skin and a wealth of mahogany hair that she wears in loose tresses. Sometimes, she even pins back tendrils at the sides with sprays of flowers. The style is oh so rustic, if you consider the current intricate fashions that involve strings of pearls and semi-precious stone beads in a dizzying profusion, but I like it. In fact, prefer it, and I would give my right hand for the opportunity to twist those beautiful curls between my fingers. Gently, of course. Cael says her preference for simple hairstyles makes her appear as if she has pretensions of being a shepherdess, but as stated earlier, he's not qualified to make an assessment of beauty when he likes his women with bleached streaks in their hair that have been stained in unnatural shades of alchemical green.

Yet Alessandra's eyes – and I have been close enough to see them on five occasions – they are a startling hazel; the pigment close to her iris a red ochre that is almost scarlet, that contrasts with the pale emerald of the outer edges. Cael says it makes her look like a vampire, but considering that neither of us has ever seen a vampire, I'll disregard his opinion once more. In any case, I'm certain vampires don't exist.

While I am an imperfect judge of fashion, I must pass some commentary on Alessandra's sense of style. Not for her the tightly cinched waists and voluminous skirts that are currently all the rage. While there is no denying that her waist is indeed narrow, she does not wear a corset so tight that it appears as if her breasts are about to burst forth in all voluptuousness. Oh, her breasts are lovely, but she does not flaunt them like a pair of overripe fruit ready for the plucking. Besides, as my mother has always said, more than a handful is a waste. Cael says she's flat-chested, yet I am equally certain I don't have a taste for boys, and I will assert that there's just enough for me to cup in each hand. Should I have the opportunity, that is. And not that I would foist myself on her person in such an uncouth fashion. I have some manners.

Cael loves to remind me that I am wasting my time pining after Alessandra, that there are dozens of young women more eminently suitable to be recipients of my affection that I don't need to moon after untouchable paragons of feminine beauty far beyond my reach or status, but I don't care.

Cael says a great deal of things, and he's welcome to his opinion, which as my mother loves to say are like bungholes. Everyone has one, and they are many and varied. I am allowed to adore Alessandra, even from a distance, for there is no wrong in looking upon that which is rich in beauty – much as one would gaze upon fine paintings and sculptures in a gallery. Beauty feeds the soul, and the gods alone know that there is so much that is brutish and awful in the world these days that we need all the beauty we can extract from our lives. Not that I visit many art galleries, but the sentiments are there.

Even I, but a lowly foot soldier for one of Ardent's Shadow Princes, should enjoy the privileges of those who walk in the sun. No matter that Alessandra's father is one of the great Sun Princes. I'm well aware that such a match that I yearn for is ill-starred and impossible. Our love is dream stuff, and it nourishes my heart when all around me is ugly and broken.

Cael says I should read fewer serials, and besides, that reading will fill my head with unattainable aspirations. I tell him it's the dreams that keep us alive and give our existence meaning. I do not adhere to any of the Saints and the gods that they have brought forth shining from the Dark, but I do know that if I were a Saint, then Alessandra would be my goddess, and I would kill even the Bull of Yarga for the privilege of bathing her feet in the sacred tears of the moon.

I live for the Day of the Bells, for it is when all the towers and steeples across the delta celebrate dawn with tongues of brass, and my heart rejoices, for I shall see my goddess at noon.

\*

Today is no different from any other Day of the Bells. Cael and I finish our rounds at the Copper Wharf, having collected from the coppersmiths who owe fealty to our family. Cael has that tight smile he always gets once we're done. He knows where we're headed. He also knows better than to complain – it's been this way for six months now.

The Library of Doves is on the southern side of the isle, which means it receives more of a breeze, and during midsummer this stirring makes all the difference to the muggy, soupy air. The library is skirted by one of the older public gardens – a pleasant, terraced affair where many visit during the noon hour. Vendors sell iced treats, fruit teas, and flavoured wines, and it is altogether preferable to find a patch of grass or if you are lucky, a coveted bench by a cheerful fountain or watercourse. While viridian peacocks spread their many-eyed fans for their intended loves, many people will do the same, after their fashion, although in our case I'd say it is the female of the species who is brighter than the male.

Cael and I are drabber than most, garbed as we are in our black tabards and trousers that mark us as belonging to one of the Shadow Princes. It is not so much that ordinary folk give us a wide berth – for that is also the case if we are within spitting distance – but it also allows for a degree of anonymity. Gazes skate past, as if those present could unsee us. As per our designation, we melt into the shadows better. Which is why my beloved Alessandra has never had the opportunity to truly see me.

My lady has already stationed herself at her accustomed spot by the statue of Narcisse. Every Day of the Bells she sits here for exactly half an hour so that she may sip a berry ice while glancing through the books she has borrowed from the library. This is the time Cael usually stretches himself out in the shade with his wide-brimmed hat pulled over his face.

He says this is because he cannot abide to see me salivate over my princess. We both know it's because he needs a snooze after he's smoked one of his roll-ups. His predilection for noon-hour traveller-weed makes him sleepy-eyed and dull. He says I should consider taking up the habit as it will a more healthsome fixation than Alessandra.

Today, however, is perfect. A whisper of a breeze stirs – enough to cool the skin of my face. While Cael is supine and snoring softly, I sit with my legs dangling over the terrace wall, ostensibly gazing down towards the Copper Wharf. I'm not the only one doing this, so it does not seem untoward. Alessandra has seated herself beneath the star magnolia, slightly to my left and on the terrace just below ours. From where I sit, I have a perfect view of the graceful arc of her neck. Her hair is pulled over her left shoulder, and she has a spray of lilac bird-eyes pinned just above her ears. The two men-at-arms who are her escort stand with their backs to us. They, too, are gazing across the delta into the distance, where the Azure Sea is lost in a haze. No doubt they are discussing the boat races or what they will do later, when they return to their barracks. One of them has lit a pipe, which the pair shares. A faint scent of burning cherry reaches me, and I wrinkle my nose. I'm not much one for any smoke. In my opinion, it dulls the senses.

In my daydreams, I approach Alessandra, perhaps with a bunch of hand-picked summer flowers, and she'll invite me to seat myself next to her. We'll talk about our lives, about the latest musicals, about...

This is where I'm stumped, for I cannot fathom what she'll want to talk about. Cael is right: our lives are too vastly different. She lives in a palace on a stretch of the Ardent delta where the banks are furred with reeds. Me? I live in a musty tenement on the top floor of a leaning block where a tepid breeze stirs ragged clothing on lines stretched across the street. Here the street urchins are as likely to stab you for the copper in your purse as they are to kick a bundle of rags between makeshift goal posts.

Besides, as Cael loves to remind me with great relish, what could such a fine lady have to do with a man who owes a year's worth of gambling debts to a house of ill repute? And he is right. Not only that, but it has been common news for three weeks now that my beloved is betrothed to Leonidas Delaroche, heir to the great Delaroche family. What hope do I have? My word is not one that can send a dozen merchant ships to the four quarters, to return laden with spices, furs, and silver. So I remain seated on the wall, engaging in make-believe, while the lady of my heart sips delicately at her beverage and turns the pages of her books. For half an hour each week, I'll bask in the light of her countenance, and that must be sufficient to nourish me for the six other days where I am grubbing in the muck.

# CHAPTER 2

Later, we wend our way down to Dog's Row on the Isle of Pillars. It's a nasty little district wedged between the warehouses by the docks and an ancient quarry full of dank water. Not even the indigent will hole up on its shores, for stories abound of things that lurk among the palsied reeds that choke the water's edge.

If members of our family have had to send a few troublemakers to sleep there with stones filling their pockets, they never tarry once the deed is done. Everyone who's been there after dark has spoken of a sense of being watched, and not by something savoury. We're not exactly savoury, you dig? So for us to feel ill at ease suggests that there is something out there that has sharper blades. Or longer teeth.

But I digress. Dog's Row consists of a narrow block of four- or five-storey row-houses that date back to the

Carolinian era – so give or take about three or four hundred years ago. Their basements are filled with water, and the walls are stained with mould. But on the top floor of number seventy-three there's also a most excellent public house where the city guard rarely bother to visit. And, most importantly, they don't water down their drinks.

Cael and I traipse up the narrow stairs, each footstep eliciting a fearsome groan or squeak from the wood. From the gloomy stairwell, the happy rumble of our friends reaches us, carried along by smoke and tang of spilled beer. It's not an altogether unpleasant smell, and I can already taste the honeyed ale I've promised myself before we head back to report in with our boss.

We halt at the doorway before entering the room.

"I think we should find somewhere else to wet our lips," I tell Cael.

I count at least a score of the Cordo family's men. While they also pay homage to our superiors – the Coltels, who control a fifth of the delta – they are not our friends. The Diamas – that's me and Cael – and the Cordos have had their fair share of skirmishes over the years. Nothing serious enough for out-and-out war, but pretty damned close at times.

Cael turns to me with a frown. "Oh, grow up. We've done nothing wrong. This is as much our spot as theirs. Make like you don't notice, and they'll leave you alone."

I grumble to myself and pray that he is right, but to my increasing discomfort, the only table available to us is right next to the big round one where six of the Cordos are seated. And I recognise Loren, who is something of a big fish among the family enforcers. If I could shrink to the size of a rat, I would, but Cael shoots me a sharpish look, and we take our seats.

"This is not a good idea," I mutter darkly.

Cael leans forward and pushes a tendril of muddy brown hair behind his ear. "Behave as if it is nothing. Can you imagine if word starts spreading that Diama men shrink from Cordos like little girls seeing a snake?"

He has a point. "Fine. Just get us something to drink, and let's make it quick. I do not wish to associate with these buffoons any longer than I absolutely have to."

Cael rolls his eyes and gets up with a groan. "Don't do anything stupid," he hisses.

"Don't worry, I'm not planning to."

The bar is thronging with men buying drinks, and the bawds offering their wares, and I have little hope that Cael's return will be quick. In the meantime, I try to sit without rounding my shoulders, and make a show of finding the wood grain of my much-scarred table unutterably fascinating. Over the years, patrons have not only carved their names on its surface, but someone has etched a rather well-proportioned naked lady. And cocks and balls. Many cocks and balls. In fact, the chair upon which I sit has a big cock and balls scratched into it.

Considering how closely jammed our seating arrangements are, it's also impossible to avoid overhearing the conversation coming from the Cordo table. For a few minutes, I try to filter it out, but then a name brands itself in my ears: Delaroche. Followed by Luciente. And oily laughter. I stiffen, hardly daring to breathe.

"Oh, she's a choice morsel all right. I reckon her father will cough up the silver, and if not him, then the golden boy shall." It's Angelo. While we're not exactly on a first-name basis with each other, I do know enough about his reputation to cross over to the other side of the street when I see him.

He specialises in kidnapping and extortion. His particular quirk involves sending bits of his hapless victims' extremities as proof to encourage payment. Icy cold fingers thrill down my spine, and I can't help but think of Alessandra's delicate hands turning pages in books.

Yet I don't dare to so much as glance in Angelo's direction. Much in the same way you don't make eye contact with a rabid dog. If I could stretch my ears to hear more, I would, but their conversation drifts to another job they completed two weeks before, and how much gold they extracted from a scion of the Suli family. They laugh about how they brushed off all attempts to exact revenge after. The webs between families, Sun and Shadow, as well as the many Gods and their Saints, is vast and complicated. Who knows who paid off whom or had a quiet word to quell imbalance. Bruised egos and missing digits aside.

Cael chooses this moment to plonk down a tankard, but what thirst I possessed earlier has fled, even though my tongue is so dry I could use it to sand down a plank.

"Who's danced on your grave now?" Cael asks with a laugh. He tips back his drink and takes three great gulps, and all I can do is turn my tankard round and round.

"Nothing."

He leans forward. "Oh, you can't lie to me, brother."

"I've heard something that fills me with great dread," I murmur then glance meaningfully to the Cordos before locking gazes with Cael.

"Oh, pray tell?" His smirk tells me that he's not taking my evident distress seriously.

"They're planning to take *her*. Tonight, I think."

A small frown mars Cael's brow, and he sits back, takes another long pull of his tankard, then sets it down and wipes his mouth with the back of his wrist. "It's none of our business."

It feels as if my eyes want to bulge out of my skull. "What do you mean 'it's none of our business'? You know what *he* does to his victims, right?"

"So? What can the two of us do? Step in a hornet's nest? It's out of our hands. We're the ones who follow orders. Unless we want to end up in the Ardent feeding the fishes."

Sudden terror squeezes my gut. It's not difficult to imagine Angelo's oily laughter as he manhandles Alessandra. How will he do it? Will he use a hatchet, or a butcher's knife?

"Benedetto!" Cael only says my full name when he's deadly serious.

I glare back at him.

"*We* can't get involved. *You* can't get involved. This is between her family and *theirs*." He glances meaningfully at the others. "Can you imagine what will happen if we overstep our bounds? We'll finally start a war between families that will destroy us all. They already hold far more territory than we do, and if they so much as sneeze, they can crush us."

I grip my tankard hard enough to turn my knuckles white. My throat is so tight not even a whimper can escape. Cael grabs my wrist and squeezes so that I'm forced to look him in the eye.

"*Do you understand?*" he hisses.

I allow myself the barest nod. However, I don't understand. Why now? Why her? Though I don't know whether I should thank or curse the Saints for placing me here at this time so that I am privy to this ill news. On most days, I am not much one for believing in destiny and the whims of Gods, but today I am filled with the passion that I have been guided, and that a great task has been laid on my shoulders.

Cael still watches me with a leery eye, but I drink deeply from my tankard. I'm going to need all the courage that I can get.

# CHAPTER 3

I say precious little all the way back to our headquarters in Bookbinders Close where we hand over our takings for the day. Cael has awkwardly filled the space between us with inanities about the boat races, about a new whorehouse out near the Southern Pier, about a shipment of wine that's being served at a tavern we sometimes frequent.

His words spill over me, around me, and trickle away because I'm lost in a fog of anxiety, barely aware enough of my surroundings to step over dog shit in the narrow streets. Maximus, our accounts keeper, reminds us of the family meeting later, and not to be late, and Cael answers for both of us as I stand by the narrow window overlooking the courtyard. Dimly, I'm aware of coins being counted, and Cael reciting who's paid what. Me? I stare at a lone dandelion growing out of a crack in the window ledge. Such a fragile gold bloom, already furling for the night. In a day or two, it will be a powder puff scattered by the wind.

Alessandra is no dandelion, but she can be crushed just as easily by someone who does not appreciate her beauty, her grace. My resolve, that has been swirling in the murk of worry and indecision up until now, crystalises in that instant. I must do the unthinkable, the one thing that I swore I'd never do – I must visit her at her father's palace. Get there before Angelo does.

A hand clamps on my shoulder, and I give a small, almost girlish shriek.

"Ben!" Cael says. "Stop wool gathering!"

"What's up with him?" Maximus says with a throaty chuckle.

"He thinks he's in love," Cael sneers. "Come, brother. We've got a few hours to kill. Let's go see about those ladies I was telling you about."

I shake loose from him and turn to Maximus. "We done here?"

He shrugs, sweeps piles of silver into pouches. "We have been done here for nearly ten minutes, boy. So unless you have something meaningful to say, I suggest you get on your way."

Cael glares at me in a way that suggests it's my fault we haven't move on yet.

"I need to go home," I tell him. "I need to...rest." Then I hurry downstairs and into the courtyard. Afternoon shadows are growing long, and if I move quickly, I can reach the Luciente palace within the hour.

But Cael's right on my heels, and before I can take two steps, he's spun me around.

His eyes are wide. "Whatever it is that you're planning, brother, don't do it."

I try to shrug him off, but he's holding onto my

sleeves so tightly I'm in danger of tearing the fabric. "I'm not planning anything." My voice comes out all wrong.

"Don't be an idiot. I know when you're lying."

I grab him by his tabard, and we stand at an impasse. "I am not going to do anything stupid." This time I'm able to get the words out in a firmer tone. "I promise."

"Every time you say 'I promise' it's because you're lying. I need you to give me your oath."

"No." I shake my head. "You know I won't do that."

Cael shoves me away hard enough for me to stagger. "You're a fool! I don't know why I put up with this shit. Every bleeding week. And for what? For this idiocy? Fine. Do what you must do, but for the love of all the Gods and their Saints, don't get yourself killed. And don't start a war none of us can win."

"I won't!" I spit. "No thanks to you."

He brushes past me, striding quickly through the entrance into Piper Street, and then he's gone in the press of late-afternoon traffic.

I should feel like shite because I've pissed him off enough for him to storm off like that, but all I feel is relief – that I can continue unhindered, without Cael yapping in my ear about this being a bad idea.

Of course it's a bad idea, and I have no clue what I'll do once I reach the palace.

\*

The Luciente family lives on a small isle on the eastern side of the delta. I hire a gondola that brings me as far as the Bridge of Hearts, where I disembark. The eastern isles exist in stark contrast to the Ardent centre. Here the banks of the river are reed-choked, and the waters run clear and unstinking. Granted, I still don't want to swim here – even during early summer when the Ardent is still swollen with meltwaters from upcountry. By early spring even this place will reek to the high heavens, and most sensible Princes will move their families to their country estates further inland or go stay at their beach villas on Crescent Bay.

There's also far less traffic for me to blend into now, and my clothing will be a dead giveaway. A foot soldier of the Shadow has no place among the wealthy. Which is why I wait for the gondola to depart, and then instead of taking the stone steps up to the bridge, where a guardsman will no doubt ask me to state my business, I slip into the reeds.

The first thing that happens is that my boots fill with muddy water. Cold water, that tells me all about the river – a brown, vegetative smell that will cling to me for days after. But I suck in a breath and start sloshing as quietly as I can along the verge until I find ground that is firm enough to tread upon while remaining hidden among the dense reeds.

It's a different world among the tall spears that hiss at my passing. I can't see for shit apart from the endless stems, and the only way I can tell that I'm not about to plunge into the river proper is by gauging the depth of the muddy water as it seeps into my footwear. Small creatures – snakes, frogs, baby crocodiles, who knows – slither off as I approach. I pray that I don't meet a white-lip viper. If one of those bite me, I may as well sit down somewhere comfortable and wait for Lady Death to collect me in her black gondola.

The Luciente palace is situated three properties ahead. Or around, if I am to be completely correct in my description. I've never called here before, but I've asked discreet questions from delivery men, so I know exactly where to go. Cael says I'm no better than a cat-sneaker having done so, but he's not here now to flap his tongue in my ear now, is he?

I have one nervous moment where I scramble across an open lawn that stretches to the water, and dogs further up at the palace start barking, but I'm quick and keep low.

It must be nice to live out here, where the residences can stretch their arms without rubbing shoulders with the next building. Each palace is surrounded by verdant parklands filled with trees and huge swathes of lawn punctuated by ornamental ponds and statues of legendary figures. The Luciente palace is a terraced confection of white columns, and it sports not one but three small domes.

From where I crouch, the building only just peers out at me from above a small forest raised by an artificial mound to offer a measure of protection when the Ardent floods during midsummer. It breaks my mind to consider how much silver has been sunk into the landscaping and construction. Someone evidently likes trees, too, and I silently thank them for not having naked lawns running all the way to the small dock with its boathouse, where a gilded gondola is moored. A pretty folly made up of graceful wrought-iron arches and topped with a conical, red-tiled roof stands on a small finger of land that juts out into the channel, and I head there because it offers me slightly better accommodation than the vegetation. Besides, I'd like to empty the water out of my boots before I press on, and that's not going to happen if I continue lurking shin-deep in the reeds.

Now what?

Low male voices reach me, and I duck behind the railing. My swimming is all right, but I have no desire to soak myself even further in river water. When I peek around the entrance, I glimpse two men-at-arms strolling along the narrow path that runs along the water's edge. Their tabards boast the Luciente flaming torch in gold on blue, and they pause a short while at the boathouse before they move past the treeline.

Idiot. That's what I am. Who am I to think that coming here will do any good? The property is guarded. She should be safe. But Angelo has a reputation – ill or well deserved depending on who you talk to – and whether he will pluck her from the very heart of the palace or waylay her while she is out in the city, I simply don't know. The way he was talking, it sounds like it could happen tonight. Which doesn't leave me with much time. The need to do something other than hunch here like a depressed mud puppy has me shifting impatiently.

When I'm sure I'm completely alone, I make my way to the path the men-at-arms followed, except I head in the opposite direction. Most likely this will win me half an hour or so, by my reckoning, depending on how often they make their rounds. Silently, I keep thanking the landscaper for more dense vegetation. The Luciente Prince's love of privacy has gifted me with sufficient places to move undetected for a short while until I reach the primary garden.

I have to suppress a small gasp of wonder at the profusion of statuary – even a massive winged horse fighting a griffin atop a fountain large enough to drown six people. What must it be like to live here, with the ever-present tinkling of water features, the soft grass, the many beds and pots overrun with scented blooms?

In the gloaming, the palace is an inviting space, the double doors on the ground floor flung open to admit the cool evening air after a stifling day. One by one, lamps are lit higher up, but of the residents I see no one.

No doubt these people no longer see the beauty that surrounds them. What is it that Cael so likes saying? Something about familiarity breeding something or other for granted? I kinda get what he means.

Soft-footed and drawn by the strumming of a lute, I tread around the perimeter towards my left, to a section of shaped hedges and pull back with a small gasp. Seated on a bench is none other than Alessandra, outside at this hour. Her face is beatific as she plays the gentle notes of an old folk song, "The Merry River", though not an arrangement I've ever heard.

Transfixed, I watch each move of her fingers as she shifts their position on the strings with fluid dexterity that rivals the best of the performers I've seen in taverns and at festivals. A small smile plays on those coral-pink lips, a secret smile, as if all the beauty and wonder of the world is encapsulated in this one moment where the passage of time has slowed to preserve the perfection that is Alessandra Luciente making music.

That's when I step on a twig, and its resonant snap breaks this magic.

Alessandra stops her playing with a small gasp and turns to face me.

It's only then that I realise I've stepped out of the protective shadows. For how long I don't know.

"You!" she exclaims as she sets down the lute next to her.

"I— Uh..." I half back away.

"You're that young man from the gardens. The one who's always sitting on the terrace above me."

What? How? My heart is fit to burst right out of my chest with the surprise.

"Um..." I cast about wildly. From where we are situated, a hedge clipped like a giant serpent blocks the direct view from the house.

Cael has always told me that I'm too impulsive to move up in our ranks. I guess he has a point. I can't think of anything better other than pouncing on the startled young woman. Kidnapping has never been my thing, but this evening I make an exception.

# CHAPTER 4

Alessandra is surprisingly biddable when I have my dagger at her throat. She doesn't so much as squeak. "They're coming for you," I tell her as I guide her down to the boathouse, all the while praying that the guards don't stumble upon us.

"Who's coming for me?" She sounds far calmer than I'd give a woman of her quality who finds herself in the position she does now.

"The Cordos. Angelo Cordo."

"Then we should tell my father."

A choked laugh escapes me. "What's your father going to do? Angelo always gets his target."

To this, Alessandra offers a small giggle. "And you're going to protect me?"

I pull at her hair for emphasis, and though it pains me greatly to do so, I move the dagger so that the blade tickles her throat. "Silence, woman. This is for your own good."

"You haven't thought this through, have you?" A mischievous quirk of her lips follows.

"Shut. Up. Not a word further."

To this she merely raises a brow, and I swear she punctuates that arched brow with the slightest of one-shouldered shrugs.

The Gods must be smiling on us, because we encounter no one on our way to the dock. It's full dark now. Our feet have barely touched the wooden deck when she twists in my grasp. The hand holding the dagger is swiped away, and she ducks under my reach.

Bitch!

But as fast as she is, I'm on her, and we go down and roll around in the muck in a tumble of arms and legs. I hate that her pretty dress gets covered in dirt, and fabric tears, too, but what else can I do? For my pains, I'm kneed in the stomach, and she does her best to gouge out my eyes. Despite her being a woman, she's much more agile than I expected.

Yet I'm able to pin her down, and we glare at each other, breathing hard, and suddenly all too conscious of our closeness. An impasse, then. My dagger lies just out of reach, and I daren't let go of this hellion's hands nor shift to allow her movement. In another time and place, being entangled like this would be pleasurable if it weren't for the fact that she tried to blind me only moments earlier.

It's then that we hear the shouting and the cries of alarm up at the house, the clash of steel on steel. She freezes, as do I.

Alessandra's eyes widen enough for this to be apparent in the gloom. "You were not lying." Her words are breathy.

"No." I pitch my voice low. "Do you promise to do exactly what I tell you?"

"I should go to my father."

"And walk right into Angelo and his men? You would do no good."

"And you're a better option?" She huffs and tries to wriggle from beneath me.

I help her into a seated position but keep a firm hold on her right wrist. "You do know what Angelo does to his 'clients', don't you?"

She shakes her head.

"He cuts off their fingers. There'd be no more lute playing or paging easily through your beloved books once he's done with you. He usually starts with the little finger on the right hand." For emphasis, I touch the digit.

She flinches with a grimace and wrests her hand from mine. "And you seek to protect me? You were creeping around here like a burglar. Why should I trust you? How do I know that this is not some elaborate scheme?"

I roll my eyes and help smooth her skirts. Her dress is most certainly ruined. Fine aquamarine satin with a matching lace trim. Worth more than a lifetime's earnings for some of the smallfolk in the city.

"Come with me. We'll figure something out and get you to safety once things calm down. It's only a short while before Angelo and his foot soldiers realise you're not in the house or nearby, and then they'll start searching the rest of the property. And then I won't be able to protect you."

"You protect me?" she scoffs as she gets up and slaps away my hands.

I retrieve my dagger then straighten. "Like I said, you don't know Angelo."

It's at that point that we hear footsteps pelting down the gravel pathways leading to where we sit. It could be the household guards or Angelo's men. We have no way of telling. If they've found the abandoned lute, which by now they must have, it doesn't take a clever man to reason that a member of the household might've tried to flee to the dock.

Icy terror clasps my guts and squeezes. "We don't have time!" I grip her by the upper arm and steer her to the gondola.

For a moment, I fear she's going to resist, but then she shoves past me and boards the small boat with alacrity despite her skirts. I snap out of my moment of surprise and hop in after her. Alessandra casts off while I grab the pole and push us into the open water just as two men burst out of the trees.

It's dark enough that I can't make out their faces at this distance, but no man up to any good would wear such dark clothing and run about with daggers unsheathed. Besides, if they were household guards, they'd be calling out to us and not fuming at us in ominous silence from the bank. Alessandra clutches the sides of the gondola as though I am about to tip us both over.

A small spike of relief that we erred on the side of caution rather than wait for these thugs to reach us, alleviates my terror.

"Bastards," she hisses. "They'll pay for this. If they've hurt any of my family…"

I don't want to tell her this may well be the case. I pole us out quickly just as the alarm bell from the Luciente palace starts painting the air with brassy tones.

"You can drop me at the bridge," she says as she turns around. "The guardsmen will help."

"And if they've been paid off?" I tell her. "How do you think Angelo got in in the first place? He's not the sort to be mucking along the river's edge like me." I glance at my ruined boots and breeches.

"Nonsense! Those men are beyond reproach."

"Oh, so don't believe me, the one who has actual experience in these matters," I tell her.

"Me, believe a scion of the Shadows?" she scoffs.

"Right now, I'm the only one keeping you unharmed. If it weren't for my foresight in coming to warn you—" My mouth is getting away from my mind. I don't want to admit to her that I have absolutely no plan at all.

Her laughter is harsh and sudden. "So you chose to try kidnap me before they did."

"Would you rather your fingers be cut off? I was... I was going to warn you."

"But like you've said, that'd have done absolutely no good. They would have come for me anyway."

I shrug and mumble an expletive under my breath.

"Janeus's tits," she says as she settles back in the gondola. "Now what?"

"We get you to a place of safety. I have a friend who—" I shake my head. Cael's going to kill me.

"You have a friend who?" Alessandra gestures for me to continue.

"He'll know who we have to speak to so we can get you back to your family safely. And smooth over this situation."

"You are aware who my betrothed is, aren't you?"

I nod miserably. Oh, and don't I know... The whole of Ardent does.

"If he gets to hear of this..." Alessandra gives a little hiss and rubs at her grubby arms.

"There will be trouble. For everyone."

"My father will lose face. That's if he's even still alive."

"Cael will know what to do," I supply. I only hope he will. That's after he's done killing me or, failing that, flaying me out of frustration. His remonstrations are already ringing in my ears.

Alessandra looks up sharply. "And now that I have you as my dubious benefactor, I suppose I should know your name, considering that you know so much about me. And my reading habits." Her mouth is pulled into a firm line.

"Benedetto de Lyse," I inform her with the most graceful bow I can manage without losing my grip on the pole or toppling myself into the Ardent.

"That's a Cantessa surname."

"My mother was from there." I didn't add that my mother had been sold into service to a whorehouse in Ardent from a young age, and still plied her trade. Granted, she wasn't front-of-house anymore, and had taken on a more managerial position within the house, but she still had her regulars who often paid gold for her time.

"And your father?"

I shrugged. He could be anyone.

"Oh, this is just perfect. Mother will be so pleased to know that my dubious benefactor is…" She heaves a sigh and closes her eyes.

"Dubious?" I offer.

"Your diction astounds me, my Shadow prince. Last time I heard, there weren't any colleges in the underground."

There is other traffic on the waters, mostly private gondolas, but to give her credit, she doesn't call out to them, though if I could bet a half-silver, my lady has considered doing so. Midges are out in full force now that it is dark, and I do the gentlemanly thing by offering her my jacket.

Alessandra sniffs at the fabric then eyes me with severe misgivings. "You don't have lice, do you?"

"I'll have you know that I have my clothing laundered at least once a week. That jacket was cleaned only three days ago." Except that it's now muddy and smells of the Ardent. But that's currently the least of my worries.

But we both know the midges are pernicious, and to save her arms, she pulls on the jacket then tucks her hands into the sleeves, which are far too long for her, in any case.

"Your plans, master thief?"

"I have a place where you can be safe. Upon my honour as a member of the Diama family that no one will harm a hair on your head, and we will have this entire misunderstanding resolved by daybreak. In which case your affianced will be none the wiser."

Alessandra arches a perfect brow. "What gives me the impression that you possess neither the rank nor the certainty to make such bold claims?"

"You wound me." I press a hand to my chest then continue poling.

"The Gods know I'll do more than merely wound you, if given half the chance," she mutters. "Gelding isn't far from mind right now."

"I guarantee things would have been far, far worse this evening had I not intervened. As it stands, the Cordos will have their agents casting a wide net for you. They have the city guard in their pockets, and no doubt your esteemed father also has his enemies."

"Who doesn't?" she allows then catches her bottom lip in her teeth for one bewitching moment.

"Exactly," I say.

"You're such a naïve fool," she tells me, "but fine. I will go with your little scheme. For the present. And only because you claim to know more of the Shadow princes' doings than I do. Though I daresay a swift return to my father's palace would be better than this supposed 'place of safety' you claim to have."

By now we've reached one of the busier branches of

the river and share the waters with barges in addition to myriad other gondolas. We both fall silent, and I'm grateful that she's as watchful as I am, her posture upright while we scan the night for threats.

We have one bad moment where a city guard longboat slices past, the men rowing under the terse orders of their captain. Time appears to slow down as we cruise alongside them, and the captain's gaze skates over us. I look ahead of myself, despite the urge to follow their progress, and keep on pushing, while Alessandra resolutely faces me. Don't. Do. Anything. Stupid.

Then the moment is past, and I can't help but exhale a shuddery breath.

"For your sake, I hope you're correct in your assessment of my predicament," she says. "Even now, my father or mother might be injured. I should be there and not taking the air with a ruffian."

Ruffian, hah.

"Give me tonight. You have my oath as a member of the Diama family that I will do everything in my power to keep your safe." Oaths aren't given lightly. We of the Shadow princes' servants may be involved in shadowy deeds, but to break oath even if you are the sort to have blood on your hands is a worse crime. Even Angelo wouldn't give his oath without the intentions of keeping his word. Only common lawbreakers break faith. Say what you want about the Shadow princes and those who serve them, we do still maintain honour. Without it we are nothing but the muck that clings below the high tide mark in the docks.

Alessandra firms her lips. Her face is a mask, and her only tell that she's under extreme stress is the slight whitening of her knuckles when she extends her hand past the sleeve so that she can clasp my jacket closed over her collarbones.

We do not speak at all for the rest of the journey, for I must maintain vigilance every time we pass beneath a bridge or take yet another branch of the river. Above us, the mounts upon which so many buildings are stacked loom, the lights of the many residences all too golden and cheerful. Ardent is a city of artificial hills. Over the centuries that the city has existed, we've kept building new upon old, and raising our structures so that they can stand above the river's damp. As it is, most buildings on the water's level have flooded basements, and every summer, during the inundation, those of us who don't live on higher ground often suffer.

If you dig deep enough, you'll find the bones of a far older city, and it's not uncommon for curious artefacts to be unearthed whenever there are excavations. Good pickings for those of the Shadow princes who don't mind grubbing in the dirt before the Gods demand their share.

I nearly weep with relief when we make it back to Eel Wharf, which is the nearest mooring to my tenement, which is on the Isle of Salt – closest to the merchanters' docks. It's not a pretty place, and I hurry us out of the gondola and up into the press of bodies before we anyone can pay us more attention than we need.

Alessandra's all stiff, her shoulders hunched, and she says nothing when I put an arm around her narrow waist and guide her through the evening crowds. Sailors are rolling into the dockside inns, porters pulling evening shift, and dozens of students are slumming it where bawds cat-call them from the balconies of the whorehouses.

"I never thought I'd ever see this," she murmurs to me.

I give a small snort. "This is nothing. Wait until brawls pour out of the taverns into the streets. It gets far more exciting."

"I can well imagine." Is that a trace of amusement?

The moment we step between the buildings, we start ascending the narrow stairs where the commercial buildings give way to a warren of tenements. Some lean over so far that their roofs nearly nudge those of their neighbours. The gutters are dank with waste, human and otherwise, and a pang of shame grips me as I consider that I am bringing her here.

But what else can I do?

Those whom we pass are as draggled as you can expect for the Salters, as the people of this isle are known. They're a tough lot, who've seen much. Salters also give a leery eye to strangers, which provides me with even more motivation to hurry us along before someone starts asking questions I don't want to answer.

"Do you even know where you're going?" she murmurs.

"Of course," I reply. "Know this place like the back of my hand."

A cat slinks across our path, and she jerks.

"It's just a cat."

"Looked more like a rat, if you ask me."

"I'm not asking you. Now come. Down here." I steer her into the lane where my tenement's front door is. Actually, scratch that. We haven't had a front door in all the three years I've lived here. Alessandra hesitates before we enter the dark, piss-stinking maw.

"Don't even think about running," I whisper. "You'll last all of five minutes if you try to go it alone through these streets."

"I'm an idiot."

"No, you're not," I say with as much kindness as I can muster.

She turns to look at me, her lovely eyes wet with the first tears I've seen. "Why am I doing this? I should have gone to my father..."

"And then you'd be in Angelo's clutches. Trust me, please. I gave you my word. I have not harmed you yet, and you know I will do all in my power to keep you safe."

Her breath heaves, and her conflicting thoughts play across the miniscule twitches on her brow and cheeks. Then she relaxes. "All right."

"After you?" I bow towards the doorway with as much chivalry as I can muster, even though I'm dying inside. Never in a thousand eons did I ever imagine I'd have to bring the light of my life to my home. Until now, I've never been so deeply ashamed of it.

Alessandra hikes up her skirts and takes those first steps, and I follow, our footsteps muffled on the ancient wooden stairs. I'm on the top floor, and though the state of the tight passage is abysmal, I'm glad to say that I have far better standards of housekeeping within. My one room is tiny, but it's clean – my mother did impart that much good sense, for I make my bed every morning, even if it is merely an old mattress on the floor.

The candle that I light throws a cheerful, wobbly circle that causes the shadows to dance and hides the walls' dismal grey. My clothing hangs on a makeshift rack, and so far, I've managed to keep the lonesome potted fern on the windowsill alive, despite the uncertainties attached to my way of life.

Alessandra turns on one spot, evaluating my quarters. Then she heads over to the small shelf by my bed – only a plank propped up on two bricks, but it's better than making a pile of books on the floor.

"You actually do read," she says with small wonder

as she sits on my bed and reaches for my volume of collected short stories by Achilles Cruisante.

"I'm not a complete barbarian." What I really want to say is that she's the one who inspired me to lose myself in literature in the first place, but to do so would be far too gauche.

Alessandra looks up at me, and for the first time I see a small measure of hope in her eyes. "You surprise me, Benedetto." Her voice dances over the syllables of my name.

I smile. "I try, my lady. Can I offer you something to drink? I'm afraid it is only wine, and not particularly good wine at that, but I am certain that after this ordeal you could use something to fortify yourself." I don't mention that no one would willingly drink the water from this isle's wells.

For a moment I fear she will refuse, but she nods, and I go to the box where I store such victuals that I dare to keep in my room. Break-ins are not uncommon in this tenement, and I've been burgled a dozen times since I've moved in. Evidently, the Diama family name is not quite enough of a deterrent for petty thieves. Maybe in a month or two I'll get that promotion I've been hoping for, and then I'll look at finding better accommodation. For now, I make do with what I can afford.

I cringe when I hand her the battered tin mug which I've slopped half full of a vintage one step above vinegar. "It's clean, I promise."

Her laugh is wry as she accepts my offering. "At this point I have no better option but to trust you." Alessandra takes that first sip and only winces slightly before she hands the mug back to me. "I've tasted worse."

"Are you just saying that to make me feel better?" But

when I take my own sip of the liquid, I have to admit that this particular lot barely qualifies as vinegar.

"What now?" she asks.

A moment of quiet lies between us. She still has my jacket over her shoulders, and her face is smudged with mud.

"I forget my manners!" I exclaim. "You may wish to clean up."

"I don't exactly see a bathroom here."

"There isn't one, but I'll fetch you water. Cold, I'm afraid, and you'll have to use one of my clean shirts for a washcloth, but I'm sure you'll feel better. I hope."

Alessandra laughs. "I'm not planning on staying that long that I'll need a bath, but the gesture is appreciated. Thank you."

I hurry downstairs to the communal well point and just about fall over my feet rushing back upstairs, as if she's a mirage that will have vanished by the time I return.

But she's still there, staring out of my narrow window while absently stroking the fronds of the sad fern.

"I'm back!" I tell her somewhat unnecessarily as I place the water on the table then hurry over to the clothing rack where I find my second-best shirt.

She accepts it from me but still stares at me with those wide eyes of hers. "And after this?"

"I'm going to go to see Cael, my...brother."

"He's the one who's with you every time I see you outside the library, who looks like he'd rather be anywhere else?"

I nod. "He'll know what to do. Who we need to deal with."

She sighs. "I hope you're right. And what of me?"

"You can stay here. Latch the door from the inside, and promise me you'll stay put until I get back. You'll be safer here than on the streets where I have to go."

"Are you sure?"

I want to tell her that I haven't had a burglary in a month, but that's hardly going to reassure her. Besides, burglars tend to avoid places that have people in them. "You'll be fine. I won't let any harm come to you. You have my oath, after all."

"I want to believe you."

I go on one knee before her, my right hand pressed to my heart. "You have my oath."

Her sad smile says my words ring hollow. "All right, master thief. Be quick about it. We don't have all night."

# CHAPTER 5

Cael grabs me by the arm the instant I set foot in Bookbinders' Close. "Where the hell have you been?" His momentum shoves me against a wall so hard my breath escapes in a whoosh.

"What?" Playing coy with Cael never works, but that doesn't stop me from trying. It feels as if all my blood rushes to my boots.

"It's your doing, isn't it?" He presses his face right into mine, his teeth bared in a pained grimace.

"*What?*" I can't quite help the whining edge that's crept into my voice.

"It's the mother of all clusterfucks, that's what it is, and we've got you to thank for it."

"What have you said to our bosses?"

"Nothing. Yet." He lets go of me, and I sag against the wall.

"Good," I murmur. "I need you to come with me. I have

something I need to show you."

"What. Have. You. Done?" he grinds out.

"I can't tell you!" I snap. "I can only show you. You're the only person who'll be able to help me."

"We're not going anywhere just yet." He shakes his head, his smile so tight he looks constipated. "It's all swords up at headquarters. Our meeting's just gotten itself stepped up from 'regular' to 'the isle is burning', no doubt thanks to whatever it is that you want to show me."

"I can't afford to go to the meeting. I need to go—"

"If you don't show up at the meeting, it's going to go worse for you. So we're going to attend and then afterwards, we'll go see whatever it is that you want me to see."

"We *can't*, Cael." I clutch at his tabard in my desperation and get my hands slapped for the effort.

"You're a grown man. Start acting like it. Right now you look like a boy that's stepped on broken glass with bare feet."

My lungs don't want to work properly, and it feels as if my world is spinning around my head. She'll be fine. She'll be fine. She promised she'd stay there, didn't she? I go over her words and realise that she never did once promise that she'd stay.

"We don't have time," I tell my brother.

"And you will be out of the family if you don't attend the meeting. You know what they do to oath-breakers, don't you?"

"Yessss, but I gave her my word…"

"Shut up!" he hisses and slaps a hand over my mouth and presses me against the wall. "You are going upstairs, and you are going to act as if nothing is the matter. We're going to hear what the bosses have to say, and then we'll go back to your stinking hovel and deal with whatever, *whoever*, it is that's there. I don't want to know, but I have a really good idea who it is, and I don't want to get involved in this mess. But I promised your mother I'd look after you, and that's what I'm going to do. So stop your snivelling. *Now*." He shoves me hard against the wall so that my head thuds against the plaster.

I nod, inhale and exhale shaky breaths until they stop rattling against my ribs. All the while, Cael glares at me until I offer him a nod, and he all but frogmarches me up to our headquarters.

We're late, and the small meeting room is already packed with our family. We squeeze into a spot slightly to the left of the door and by the wall. I wither the moment I clap eyes on Vincent. He's our Prince's chief advisor, and it's rare for him to address the foot soldiers personally. An older man, he is dressed impeccably in a black suit with a trademark spray of wax flowers in his lapel, and he is quietly conferring with our captain. It's weird seeing so many of our family gathered – we're small fry compared to the others – two score foot soldiers, and twice as many allies among the city folk. Tonight's meeting was initially intended only for our sub-division, which meant it was me, Cael and four or five others who handle the contributions made by the businesses within our territory. But now it's a full house.

Do I regret my actions of earlier? Yes and no. This realisation helps me straighten. I may have inadvertently landed myself in a hornet's nest, but to think of Alessandra losing one of her beautiful fingers or perhaps even an ear or the tip of her nose thanks to Angelo's not-so-tender ministrations – now *that* is intolerable, and I would prefer the ire of our Prince than live with any harm befalling my beautiful love.

As if sensing the firming of my resolve, Cael nudges me in the ribs and mouths, 'Not. A. Word'. He doesn't have to worry. There's no way I will incriminate myself right now. To Vincent, I'm a nobody, the son of an associate who's trying to prove himself worthy to the family. And now I've gone and fucked myself. And the family. All I can do now is wait out this meeting then beg that Cael helps me figure out something after. Also, I don't need to be a seer to understand that I'm the very cause of why a routine meeting has morphed into something of a far bigger, more serious nature.

My heart is galloping like a spooked horse, and I have to do my utmost to breathe evenly and give the impression that I am not as guilty as a dog that's snuck links of sausages out of a butchery.

After what feels like an eternity has passed, Vincent clears his throat meaningfully, and an expectant hush settles over us. Cael nudges me hard, and I straighten. My clothing adheres to my armpits, and a cold trickle runs down my back.

"Some of you may already have heard about tonight's events," Vincent begins. "But for those of you who have missed the news, we've got a small complication on our plates."

No shit.

Muttering breaks out, but Vincent holds up his hands as though he were calming the ocean. "It would seem that someone, a freelancer or one of our rivals, has interfered in the work of our allies, the Cordos."

This is it. He knows. They all know but are just toying with me. A whimper builds in my throat, but Cael stomps hard on my foot. I swallow the small sound.

"We have been in discussion with our allies, and we have agreed to assist them in their inquiries to get to the bottom of the problem. We will be dividing our territory into sections, to which you will be allocated. Ignore no potential sources of information – we need to find out who has kidnapped the daughter of Prince Luciente. Alessandra is to be brought unharmed to Angelo Cordo so that he might complete the transaction."

I groan, and Vincent's gaze fastens onto me faster than a tomb viper to a rat.

"Do you have something you'd like to say?" Vincent asks me.

My mouth opens but no sound comes out. It's Cael who speaks for me.

"My brother here was just regaling me about the young woman's beauty just the other day, sir. This is most distressing."

Vincent gazes at me speculatively. "Indeed. I have heard about this young woman's qualities. Still, it does us no good to be distracted by pretty faces. We have work to do."

Fortunately for me, someone else, one of my brothers from the western coastal region, asks a question, and Vincent's attention shifts.

Cael glares at me in a way that suggests that not only am I a colossal idiot, but that I need to shut my yap for the rest of the evening. It's the kind of look that informs me without words that he should do all the talking from here on in. And for the following three quarters of an hour or so that particulars are imparted to us, I am content to stand behind Cael's left shoulder, all but a shadow. He and I are to patrol the docks, to ask whether the young woman has been seen embarking or even disembarking. I pray and hope that no one marked me and Alessandra when we abandoned her father's gondola. By now someone will have noticed the vessel.

This is unfortunate, and I didn't even spare this a thought at the time. Perhaps it is a good thing that we'll be wandering the area – it means I will be able to cover up this lapse in my judgment.

The air inside the tiny room grows close, and I can't tell whether it is my increasing state of nervousness that is making me feel faint or the lack of breathable air. Perhaps it is a bit of both. My eyes are growing heavy, despite the sense of desperation that burns the soles of my feet. Cael and I need to get moving, even though I can almost guarantee what his suggestion will be – to hand Alessandra over to Angelo and be done with the matter.

He speaks for both of us when it is our turn to stop by the map of the city spread out on the table. Vincent pinpoints exactly the area that we need to cover, and I hate the way his dark eyes linger over me while Cael asks questions. He must suspect, for I am unnaturally withdrawn. Usually, by now, I'd have been the butt of at least one or two good-natured jokes from my fellows.

"You all right, Benedetto?" Vincent asks. "You're looking a little piqued."

"Bad ale this afternoon," Cael answers before I can speak, and I shake my head for emphasis.

"Dog's Row," Cael supplies, as if that will explain everything.

"Ah," Vincent says. "I have not heard good things about that place lately. Perhaps it's overdue that someone puts a torch to it."

"Long past overdue," Cael affirms, and I manage to laugh weakly with him, even though I don't find the idea of arson funny at all. My mother and I once got caught in a fire when I was small. We survived by leaping into the Ardent, and it took weeks for me to recover from the fever I caught from accidentally ingesting river water.

By the time we exit, I nearly fall over my feet in relief as we traipse down the stairs. My brothers are speculating about who would be so stupid as to poach on Cordo territory and what might happen to the fool who has done so. Meanwhile, that very same fool presses his lips firmly together while he tries not to lose himself in an outright panic. They talk casually of beating the guy up, of breaking his hands and feet. My extremities ache in sympathy.

If I'd known…

And yet, when I think of Alessandra, I'd rescue her all over again, although this time I realise I should have fled the city with her and not left her holed up in my tenement. We're boxed in, and now not only are the Cordos and the city guard after us, but my own family. We're so solidly screwed it's not even funny.

Cael has nothing to say to me as we make our way down to the docks. It's only once we've slipped into a busier street where porters are heaving their loads up from the wharf, and groups of students are headed down, arm in arm and loudly proclaiming how much they're going to drink, that he speaks.

"Now you can show me what it is that you need to." Cael doesn't so much as look at me.

"I went to—"

"No! You must show me. No telling. The streets have ears. And eyes." He glances about, and if I could, I would kick myself hard in the shins.

"And you promise you'll help me."

"I'll help you do what you're supposed to do."

Ugh. I knew it.

We hurry but take a circuitous route that doubles back so that we can be certain we're not tailed. If someone is following us, they're really good, because we don't see anyone. I don't know whether I should be relieved or worried, but what I do know is that I'm about to crawl up the walls in my anguish. Every moment that I am away, means one more moment that Alessandra is alone in my room. And I didn't warn her about the mice or the roaches.

Then again, despite her gentle birth, there is a manner about her that suggests she is made of sterner stuff than an ordinary Sun-bred noble, and I cling to this notion that she won't faint dead at the first scuttling vermin.

I take the stairs in my tenement building three at a time while Cael plods up after me, because a growing horror has laid its hand upon my heart that—

My feet slide to a halt before my mind has fully registered what my eyes are telling me. My room's door, kicked off its hinges.

"Fuck."

"What?" Cael is at my side, slightly behind me because the passages in this building are too narrow for two men to stand abreast. "Oh."

Icy fear loosens my guts as I step over the splintered remains. My living quarters may be minimalist, but whoever was here went out of their way to destroy what little I own. Even my spare clothing has been shredded and left in a noisome pile, and the same arsehole who broke down my door also pissed and took a shit on my things. My small collection of books has been torn to shreds, the papers lying in sad flutters all about.

Alessandra, of course, is nowhere to be seen.

"Is this what you brought me to see?" Cael asks. "You should really think about getting a better place to stay. How many times have you been burgled now? I can recommend a spot on—"

My only fruit knife is standing to attention in the wall above my ripped-up mattress with all its straw stuffing clotted in sodden piles. But it's not so much my fruit knife that catches my attention, but the paper that it's pinning to the cracked plaster.

I tear this off then go stand by the window so some light from outside can help me decipher what has been scrawled on the sheet. My poor fern has been defenestrated, because it's no longer on the window ledge. What did the plant do to warrant such treatment? That one flyaway thought strikes me as absurd considering the bigger problems I'm facing.

"What does the note say?" Cael cranes his neck so he can peer over my shoulder.

> Most esteemed friend
> In the light of your non-payment of dues owed The House of Magnolias, we have removed your woman as surety. While her service to our illustrious establishment will go some way towards covering your debt, we strongly advise that you supply us with the silver owed. We hear that a ship from the Colonies is due to dock within the week, and there is a call for indentured servants. You're a nice, young strong man. I'm sure you can figure out your worth.
> Lisabet Pell

"You haven't paid that yet?" Cael sounds incredulous.

"No," I mumble. "I was hoping—"

The slap to the back of my head is so hard and so unexpected that my temple ricochets off the window frame.

"Ow!" I turn, rubbing at the stinging skin.

It's too dark for me to see Cael's expression, but by the set of his shoulders, he's furious. "You're doubly an idiot and a fool!"

"I know! You don't have to slap it in."

"I'll have to do more than slap it in by the looks of it. I told you to set up payment terms with these people. They're associated with the Serpentés. Our Prince cannot cover to save your scrawny arse. Why did you even go put yourself at risk like that in the first place?"

"I thought I had a winning streak…"

"Oh, for fuck's sakes. You of all people should know that the house always wins. Especially when it comes to people like you."

I clutch at my head and moan. "I know, all right. I've fucked up."

"And now they have *her*, don't they?"

I nod miserably.

Cael gives a small, inarticulate groan. "Come, I can't think in here with the stench. You're going to have to crash at my room tonight."

"What are we going to do now?" I mutter after him as we step out of my reeking former home.

He spins to face me in the passage. "If I thought you'd fucked things before this, you've doubly, *triply* fucked everything. We're going straight to Victor now, and you're going to go down on your hands and knees and grovel like you've never grovelled before, and maybe, just *maybe*, you won't end up sucking the muddy bottom of the Ardent come sunrise."

If I could seep into the floorboards and cease to exist at this very instant, it would not be enough. Angelo manhandling Alessandra is bad. What Lisabet's madams will make Alessandra do is worse. She'll be whored out to all and sundry. And what's worse, is that when word of this filters back not only to Alessandra's family but her betrothed's...

"If we were on the verge of a battle earlier, we're now at the front of an all-out war, boy. Boy!" Cael grabs me by the shoulders and shakes me. "Thanks to you."

"Let go of me!" I cry. "I'm not going to let it come to that!"

My stomach does its best to contort itself into knots, and I swallow back the sourness that rises in my throat.

"You?" Cael's laughter is incredulous. "You're only going to make things worse!"

"What do you know? This is the woman I love, and I will—"

The crack of the flat of his palm against my cheek stuns me into silence so fast I bite my tongue and taste iron.

"*Now*! We're going *right now*." He grips my tabard and

starts tugging, but I'm faster than him.

I slip out of the garment and shove past him so that he's left cursing in my wake, my clothing discarded like the useless skin the way a skink drops its tail so it can escape a cat. I'm a dead man. I may as well make every last moment count. I run, Cael's swearing ringing in my ears.

## CHAPTER 6

Now, not only do I have the Cordos sniffing on my trail – that's if they've figured out that I'm the one responsible for snatching their prey out of their grasp before their fingers closed around her – but I've my very own family hunting me down, as well. By my estimation, it will take Cael about half an hour to hurry back to headquarters, and another hour or two before the word has gone out to all our foot soldiers to converge on The House of Magnolias.

I am beyond dead. So very, very dead.

That's if they follow this particular course of action, which will no doubt lead to the Serpenté family initiating a little feud of their own. And all the Saints and their Gods help me if the Delaroche family gets involved... I do not much fancy the idea of being hung, drawn and quartered in public. The executioners are incredibly skilled and have had much practice in recent years, and I'll most likely only die at the quartering part of the torture. That's if I don't end up shipped off to the Colonies or become personally acquainted with the silty bed of the Ardent that already swirls with the sad remains of many an unfortunate.

My anxiety lends my feet wings as I pelt, jacket- and tabardless through the streets, over bridges and along lanes. I am no better than a common thief, but I still have the tatters of my honour and my oath that I will allow no harm to befall Alessandra. Even if she is cursing my name at present, it matters not. I must rescue her or die trying. I cannot bear the thought of strange men and women pawing at her, and I curse the day I gave in to the temptation to overplay my hand at Lisabet's tables.

Yes, I am an idiot and a fool. I freely admit it. But allow me to add that it was out of no desire to wilfully do ill to those I care for. Yet if war breaks out on the streets because of this, I'll be the one who has blood on his hands. Especially if Cael or any of my brothers are injured or killed.

\*

The House of Magnolias stands on an islet in that murky territory that is somewhere between the eastern isles and the docks proper – so no self-respecting scion of the Sun would establish a palace there, thanks to the location's proximity to the docks and all the activity that takes place there. Yet it's not such a bad location, for one of the branches of the Ardent flows strong and deep there before hurrying into the Azure. Some say it's an islet that exists purely thanks to the artifice of man, constructed out of sheer stubbornness to shake fists at the river's teeth.

The house itself is an old, five-storied structure built on the crumbling, terraced remnants of what may once have been a temple to one of the river gods of the days before the Saints shone their lights upon the primordial Dark, but it's impossible to tell. The only way to reach the islet is by gondola, for it stands thirty feet out into the waters.

No boatman will ferry me across with me in this state. The House of Magnolias may be a den of iniquity, but it maintains impeccable standards. Besides, during my scuffle with Cael, my purse must've come loose from my belt. I have larger problems than a few missing copper and bronze bits, and currently, as I stand on one of the piers projecting into the Ardent, it's as if I can feel my pursuers' blades already whispering on the soft skin of my neck.

Two lazy gondola men eye me from the next pier across, but neither makes any effort to hail me. They shrug, murmur to each other, and the one lights his pipe. It's as if they can smell my sorry state. No mind. For Alessandra I'm willing to brave worse than leeches and river stink.

When I'm sure the men are not watching, I slip over the side of the pier and clamber down among the slimy poles. Almost immediately, I lose my purchase and plonk into the foetid waters. Like a true son of the Ardent, I shut my mouth and pull myself up to the surface with certain strokes. Tonight, the river is lazy, but her current is still strong. I don't swim against her, but rather across, so that she does most of my work for me.

She's also far colder than I had initially expected, and I do not even want to dwell of what floats in her embrace. Any moment I worry that I'll have a nudge from one of the river sharks or even a sharptooth catfish. Our fishy predators are larger than anywhere else along the northern Azure coast, in all likelihood thanks to all the corpses that are offered for them to dine upon.

Just the other day I heard about a sharptooth that exceeded nine feet. By comparison, I'm only five foot seven… But this is not something I want to consider while I strike out for the islet. By the time I drag myself into the sludgy reeds at the north side, my lungs are burning, and

I've accidently ingested a mouthful of mucky water. If I don't get a second smile slashed across my throat tonight, a large chance exists that the fever might get me instead.

But while I still live and breathe, I do so for Alessandra.

Lisabet maintains stepped gardens around her property – another reason why her establishment is popular. On the south side is a view clean across the Azure, and allegedly on good nights one can see the famed lighthouse of Arminth. Tonight is not a good night, because a foul mist has risen from the river, bringing with it swarms of midges that like nothing better than to suck my blood. I've barely crawled five paces into a stand of bamboo when I can feel the little fuckers nip at the exposed skin of my face, neck, and hands. Come dawn, I'll add a rash of welts to my list of woes.

Laughter and music drift down from one of the terraces above, drowning out the lapping of water and my squelching boots. Already my heels are rubbing raw within my footwear, but this is something I can bear. My biggest concern is how I'll enter the house. Lisabet's guardsmen are not the sort to be trifled with.

I've got this far, and I still don't have a plan. I can't simply stroll in among the guests looking the way I do. Even if I were dressed appropriately, I'd still be stopped at the front door and marched directly to Lisabet's office.

Slowly, and trying my best not to make any sounds that will be heard over the celebrations, I inch along the bottom terrace. The ground here is soggy, and it's highly doubtful that any guests would ever make their way down here, but a narrow path consisting of evenly placed steppingstones follows the water's edge. No doubt the guardsmen will use this when they conduct their perimeter patrol. No guardsmen...yet... but I listen out for the soft scrape of boot leather on stone as I follow the path, then slip up the stairs to the next terrace. Here thick hydrangeas push their violet and blue blooms to the sky. They're large enough that I can drop onto my hands and knees and crawl between the vegetation.

My hand come down on manure, on soft, slippery bodies that could only belong to slugs. But things could always be worse, so I muffle my distaste for whatever it is that I come into contact with, and I keep crawling. Any moment I expect someone to call out alarm, but the longer I remain undetected, the happier I am. A savvy tracker might note the disturbed mud where I pulled myself out of the river, or the fresh boot prints imprinted in the muck near the path. I need to get in and out before dawn. Or before my people arrive. One or the other.

Doubt niggles at me, asking how I'll manage to get Alessandra off the islet. I'll figure it out, surely. I've got this far on sheer dumb luck. Or rather no luck at all, just floundering from one bad situation to the next. I hesitate, my chest tight from the fear that courses through my veins. Just what the hell is it that I think I'm doing? I should crawl back to the river now and let the current sweep me to the docks proper, where I can stow away aboard a ship and end up in the Colonies or somewhere very, very far away from this accursed city.

Maybe return in a few years' time when everyone has forgotten my name. Maybe try make my fortune as a privateer. Anything is better than this foolhardy venture I'm attempting. But my thoughts wheel right back to Alessandra, who is no doubt being readied to service a drunken client who has absolutely no idea that he is about to sully the most loveliest of visions with his pawing hands and drooling lips. That thought alone is enough to put fire in my marrow and straighten my spine.

I make it to the third terrace, having just avoided two young men locked in a furtive embrace in an artfully constructed grotto, when I encounter a door set in the wall. Someone has gone to a lot of trouble to make this look as though it isn't here, for a sheet of ivy falls over most of it, but the dead giveaway that this is an entrance that is often used comes from the fact that the wet earth at the bottom has signs of being recently smoothed over by the opening and shutting of the door. Also, there is no muck on the hinges, and the large metal ring shaped like a serpent eating its own tail, is dust free. Polished, in fact, by the touch of many hands.

A hidden entrance, of course.

Fortunately, my lockpicking set is still tucked in its pouch on the thong around my neck. I may not be the fighting type, but I do have talents that make me useful to the Diama family. While I keep an ear out for any approaching guardsmen, I set about working the lock. Here the Maiden of Fortune is once again smiling on me. The mechanism is an antique that fell out of favour half a century ago. Anyone who has anything precious they want to keep safe won't use this design. A determined five-year-old armed with the right tools and a little patience can get past this lock.

I can't help but grin when the tumblers fall into place with a satisfying clatter-clack, and the door snicks open. Well-oiled hinges, too. It's darker than the arse of the Dark itself here, and the warm, musty air that rushes out to greet me sings me a song of rising damp and things that have died many, many years ago. Things that may once have walked on two legs and pissed off the wrong people.

All right, so the old bird has a dungeon. I fill myself with even more resolve not to end up as mouldering bones in a dingy cell. With a last glance over my shoulder, I open the door just enough to slip into the gloom, feeling ahead with one hand while I slowly shut the door behind me.

I suppose now's not the time to complain about how

much I hate the dark. Absolute darkness – the kind that is oily and feels like it's slipping down your nose and throat and will eventually throttle you with its solidity. With the names of the Saints of Light under my tongue, even if they're just fanciful tales for the overly pious, I all but crawl up the dozen or so stairs. Every moment I fear that my questing fingers will come into contact with something moist and squishy or have a creature with too many legs scuttle across my wrist. My breaths huff far too loudly, and I discover that the passage appears to have been made for dwarfs, for I have to half crouch as I make my gradual ascent. After what feels like an eternity, I reach another barrier. Wood. I fumble about until my hand encounters another ring set in the wall. An experimental tug reveals that this is also locked, and I curse silently. Fortunately, I can pick locks blindfolded, and this mechanism is the same as the one below. Though it takes me a little longer in the dark, I'm gratified when I work this lock and it eventually lets go of its secret combination of tumblers.

By now I can't decide if I'm soaked through with the river water or sweat. My hands are trembling, and I swear a casual listener will be able to hear my pulse thundering its terrified tattoo.

From what I can tell, I've entered a chamber. Thin bars of light stream in from an air shaft's grille at the top where the ceiling meets the wall ahead of me, and my eyes are so accustomed to the lack of illumination that this is enough for me to discern that I've found myself inside a storeroom. The faint carrion stench is a little stronger here, and when I move towards three coffin-shaped boxes in the one corner, I have a good idea what I'd find inside them. That's if I were to lift the lid. I may be a gambling man, but I'm not *that* inquisitive. So claims of Lisabet interring her enemies alive may not be completely groundless. I should be so lucky – she's only threatening to sell me to the Colonies, where I'll no doubt break my back tending silkworms or chopping timber.

A door to my left is more solidly constructed and appears to be padlocked from the outside.

"Mother of All!" I mutter and give one last shove. I may as well be trying to shoulder a mountain. I should have expected this. I've come so far and now this?

Apart from the door down to the passage, there is no other exit unless...

I eye the air shaft. No.

Except Alessandra...

With a grimace, I head over to the stinking coffins which are conveniently placed to form steps for me.

"Sorry," I mumble to their deceased occupants as I step with first one then another boot. The wood gives slightly beneath my weight but mercifully doesn't splinter.

The air shaft is narrow, but then again, I'm not exactly built. Cael says I'm scrawny and have a girlish figure, but I think he just likes to have me on. Girlish figure or not, if I get the grille off the shaft, I should be able to worm my way through to the next room. The floor is at eye level, and the light is better here. Clay jars and barrels are visible. More storage, then. I measure the dimensions with my fingers, and it already feels as if an invisible fist is squeezing my chest.

"Oh, come on, Ben, you had to do worse when you escaped through the drainage system in Count Phillipus's palace."

But saying these small words of encouragement do little to quell the horror blooming in my gut. Just because I can do something doesn't mean that I enjoy doing it, and contorting myself like a boneless lizard doesn't exactly rate highly on my 'to do' list of enjoyable pastimes.

To add to my woes, the screws holding the grille in place have rusted into nasty little globs, so I waste precious time scraping with a blade until they eventually give. By then my fingers are raw, and my nerves have been whittled down to a knife's edge. Yet I exhale a huge gusty sigh of relief when I pull away the grille and place it onto the coffin by my feet.

Oh Gods, this is going to be horrible.

On days when he's grumpier than usual, Cael says I should have considered a career in the circus rather than a life in the Shadows. I remind him that I don't like being stared at by strangers – hence me having accepted my current career path. Besides, I don't like the idea of living in a caravan and traipsing all over the land. I'm pretty sure they'll also get me to muck out the animal cages, and I don't like bears.

I stretch as best I can, then begin. The problem most people have with movement is that they're accustomed to only a finite series of extensions throughout their day—they stand, sit, walk, lie down. And their muscles get lazy. It's not so much that the bones won't oblige, but rather that the bits that hold the bones together aren't used to doing what appears impossible. Granted, I've not exactly been keeping myself limber of late, but when I was younger my work had often involved wriggling down chimneys or up drainpipes for the family. Even if I'm unpractised, my body still remembers. The only thing I truly loathe about the process is that sense of being squeezed while suffering the very real fear that I might get stuck.

Not to mention that feeling of the weight of a building constricting from all sides, though I gain a small pleasure from the knowledge that the air shaft is most certainly not a chimney or a drain, so I won't feel like I'm being swallowed down a solid gullet. I still have nightmares about a few of the tight spots I've found myself in the past. They're the kind of nightmares where I wake with a strangled cry on my lips.

This air shaft is no joke, however. I reach the section where the broadest part of my chest becomes firmly wedged, and because one arm is still tucked at my side, I only have my right with which I can scrabble for purchase. My boot toes can't quite help with enough leverage, and for several seconds I'm stuck halfway with a ballooning panic making my chest expand uncomfortably. Even as the curtain of panic descends, I exhale, rotate. Buttons pop, fabric tears, and I rasp a little forward, and then again. My shoulders burning, I flop about until I feel the pressure ease down my ribs. I'm going to make it!

Once my hips are through, I give myself a moment to catch my breath and take stock. A small brown mouse skitters past and pauses a handspan from my face. He's so close I can look him right in his beady little black eyes. Whiskers twitch, then he scampers off into the shadows. My lungs are bellows, and I swear I will never put myself through this sort of ordeal again. I'm not six anymore. I'm way too old for this shit.

The music is louder now, as is the muted laughter and talking. I fancy I can hear wheels spinning in the gambling chamber. With a groan I rise to my knees and then to my feet, a hand positioned on a crate to steady me. Even now I can still feel the phantom pressure of the air shaft. I glare at the aperture but can't help a small grin of triumph. Mother will laugh if I ever get around to telling her about my achievement. She doesn't exactly approve of my exploits, but she has to concur that it's better than me pursuing a career as a dockhand or a common thug. And I'm not pretty enough for the whorehouses. There Cael and my mother are in agreement.

Small windows to my right offer a view to the garden, and a heavy latticework of metal trellis ensure that even if someone were to break the dusty glass, they'd have to waste precious time removing the security measures.

Additionally, the door here is heavily barred from the inside, which suggests it is only ever opened by someone already within the house.

On soft feet, I pad to the interior door on the other side. This one is only locked. That's when I reach for my trusty pouch and curse. My shirt is open, and my pouch, which has always hung around my neck, is gone.

"For the love of fucks!" I grate out then go back to the air shaft. I kneel and stick my head into the stinking dark, but now that my eyes have grown accustomed to the light in this next storeroom, I can't see for shit in the coffin room. A cursory search on the floor doesn't reveal anything either.

Fortunately, I do have a few pins and wires stashed in my boots for just such an occurrence, and using a combination of tools, I'm able to jiggle the lock. It just takes longer, especially since I'm shaking from helpless fury. I've had that particular set of tools since my sixteenth birthday. Cael gave it to me when I graduated to a full member of the family.

Before I open the door, I press my ear to the wood and spend a while listening for any tell-tale signs of people beyond. It will do me no good if I barge straight into a staffroom or the Saints forbid, right into the midst of guests. There's no way I'll ever be able to explain my sorry state – stinking of river muck, covered in dust, and with my clothing in tatters.

When I'm certain all is well on the other side, I open the door a crack and peep out. Oh, good. A passage, and a simple one at that. Stone floors and hooded gas lamps at long intervals. This must be a service corridor, and from where I stand, it looks like it merely heads off to a T-junction about six paces ahead. A few crates and barrels are stacked here, too, and I slip out and shut the door behind me.

Now what?

I'm well acquainted with the public rooms on the upper terraces, but I don't know much about the inner layout that is not open to general scrutiny. The House of Magnolias is built like a stepped pyramid, which means the further down you go, the larger the warren of passages and rooms. Even if it's inadvsiable, considering my run of rotten luck, I'm willing to bet my soul that there's more beneath the surface here than I can guess. That's if they've been able to seal against the Ardent's damp.

Which means that Alessandra could be anywhere.

There's nothing for my situation but to continue and hope against all hopes that I'm able to do so while escaping detection.

From my experience, the whores are on the floor second from the top of the house proper, and not just the ruins it projects from – the top floor being where Lisabet maintains her quarters. The floor below the whores' rooms is where the VIPs congregate, and below that is the common area most mortals with the right money partake of the pleasures of the house.

Which means I'm most likely four or five levels below even that.

My initial exploration suggests that my current level consists of a square passage that follows the perimeter of the terrace. Doors and passages open to my left and right at regular intervals, and I can only wonder what's down some of them, since not all of them are illuminated – and my current route only economically so.

Sound carries strangely down here. At times, it feels as if the music is right around the corner. At other moments, I can only hear my own footsteps. What I hate the most – apart from not knowing about Alessandra's well-being – is that I have no idea when and where I will encounter guardsmen. Despite the deathly quiet in this seemingly abandoned passage, there's precious little dust, and I can only assume that at some point a guardsman or two will pass by on their rounds. Only a fool would not patrol their own house, and Lisabet is no fool. You don't get to operate a house of ill repute so brazenly in Ardent unless you have the resources to hold onto whatever power you've been able to grasp.

After two turns to my right from the left-hand branch of the T-junction, I come to a set of stairs that lead up. They're well lit, and I wait for a few moments listening, my heart in my throat. There's no doubt that the higher I ascend, the more chance I'll either run into servants or guardsmen, yet I can't put this off indefinitely. The night will not last forever.

I take those first steps, but I don't know who's more surprised as I run straight into a woman carrying a bucket and mop. Sudsy water spills as we both shriek like small children. We stare at each other, chests heaving, and then she recognises that I have absolutely no business being here.

"What?" she exclaims as she swings at me with the mop in a way that makes it impossible for me to duck in time.

The soggy end smacks me square in the face and the foul taste of mucky water and soap fills my mouth. Unfortunately, it is at this moment that I also lose my footing, and if it weren't for the fact that I am already near the top of the flight of stairs I may have stood a chance to recover my poise.

But I was at the point of stepping, and I miss my footing. The next I know I'm tumbling down the stairs while the damnable woman shrieks fit to raise the dead. I've barely had a chance to scramble to my knees when she renews her assault. All I can do is scrabble sideways into the corner of the landing like a wounded crab, with my arms held over my head in a vain attempt to protect myself.

There's nothing quite like getting the air driven out of your lungs by a well-placed mop-strike. As I try make a break for it, men's voices echo down the passage, and if I don't move now, I'll be caught. I try to dive back the way I came, and the cleaning lady slaps my feet from under me, so that I tumble down yet another flight.

Pain is everywhere, suffusing my entire being as I lie in a groaning pile on the hard, stone floor. This is where Lisabet's thugs find me. Without even inquiring as to my state of health, they haul me up between them and drag my sorry remains along passage after passage.

"Reckon we should give Selene a promotion?" one says to the other.

The other laughs. "She'd show you a thing or two, I reckon."

I'm brought to a cell that's at least a floor below the one I've just been sneaking along, and they throw me into it. One stands by the door while the smaller of the two – mean-looking fellow with a patch over his left eye – drags me into a vaguely seated position so he can glare at me. With his free hand he searches me, and quickly relieves me of my dagger and my boot knives, which he slides to his friend.

"My, my, you are a determined one to get so far," he says, and I can hear the warped admiration in his tone.

I hurt too much to say anything.

"Check his mark," says the one by the door.

One-eye grabs my left hand and twists it around painfully.

"Diama."

"What's your name, boy?" the one by the door grates out.

"B-Ben," I stammer.

"Didn't hear that." One-eye gives me a tooth-rattling

shake so that my poor bruised head knocks against the wall, and my vision fills with stars.

"We got beef with the Diamas?" One-eye asks his friend.

"They wouldn't try sneak in like this. Not their style. Who are you, boy?"

I lick dry lips and open my eyes a crack. "B-b-benedetto de L-l-lyse."

"You heard of him?" One-eye asks Doorman.

"Nuh-uh. But bosslady will want to hear of this."

Abruptly, One-eye drops me, and all I can do is lie there in a broken heap while they shut the door, lock it, and bar it from the outside. They're not taking chances, evidently.

They don't have to worry. I am in too much pain to do anything more idiotic than what brought me here. Every breath hurts, and I wouldn't be surprised if I've cracked my ribs. Tears form in the corners of my eyes, and I blink them away. No point crying over the pain when I'll no doubt be dead soon.

# CHAPTER 7

I've failed. Unutterably. And I simply don't have anything left inside me. What little flame of desperation kept me going until now has guttered and gone out. And yet...

Alessandra.

I stir, flex first one arm then the other experimentally. My left shoulder took the brunt of that first plunge, and oh hells, it *hurts*, but I can still rotate it. This is promising. With a groan I prop myself up against the wall. My head is spinning, and warm liquid trickles down my left temple. When I probe at it carefully, my hand comes away sticky with blood. Though I don't want to find out how bad it is, I feel upward until I find the cut that's leaking. Head wounds. Ugh. They always bleed worse than anywhere else.

There's nothing I can do about it right now.

Fuck. Breathing is a bitch.

The tiny dark chamber does its best impression of swimming around me, but I feel a little better while I close my eyes and try not to breathe too hard. It's going to take weeks for my ribs to heal. I just know it. This is not the first time I've damaged the poor darlings, and in my line of work, as Cael says, I need to either get used to getting kicked or make sure I jump out of the way the next time someone wants to throw their weight around.

Gingerly, I get to my knees then rise, supporting myself against the wall, hating the way the room dances around me. In a perfect world, I should be resting up for a week or so, but that sort of luxury is a vapour dream considering my present circumstances. In all the serials I read, the hero bounces back after getting knocked on the head and is immediately able to hand the bad guys their arses. Not so in real life, as I've discovered on numerous occasions, to my detriment.

Cael says the trick is to make sure that you're not where they expect you to be, but evidently, I've yet to master that art. Not that I think I'll have further opportunities to try. But let it not be said that I give up too easily. I still have my back-up lock-picking tools in my boot, and I can, at the very least, make a start of trying to escape this hole I've dug myself.

I've only managed to get the pick into the keyhole when voices become audible on the other side of the door. With a silent curse I stash my tools and only just manage to stagger back into a seated position as my captors raise the bar, unlock the door, and push it inward. It's a different pair this time – cleaner, sterner-looking types – and they say nothing as they bind my hands behind my back with rope. With one gripping me on either side, they march me along the passages at a furious clip that has me stumbling.

"Where are you taking me?" I ask.

"Shut your yap," says the one on my left.

I err on the side of caution at his suggestion, and instead try to make sense of our route. Up two floors then to a central flight of stairs so breathlessly narrow that one man has to go ahead of me while the other shoves me from behind when I slow them down. This rough treatment does little to improve the aching of my bones and my head, and it's only when I threaten to vomit that they halt briefly to allow me to draw breath.

It's near dark here, with a dim gas lamp on each landing. A secret stairwell then, one that no doubt goes right through the heart of the structure. This is useful knowledge, if ever I have the opportunity to use it. Not that I will, but I can't help but file away the fact.

Presently, we pause on a landing and the goon in front unlatches a door then drags me stumbling into a wider corridor. Judging by the rich sheen of the polished wood floor, and the gilt-decorated floral wallpaper, we're in the mistress of the house's personal quarters. Or at least the parts that only esteemed guests get to see. I should be grateful for the honour bestowed upon me.

"What you smirking at?" the man on my left says as he gives me a good, tooth-rattling shake.

"Oh, nothing."

"Don't bait him," says my right-hand man. "I know his type. Too cocky by half. We'll see what the boss lady has to say."

That I'm right about where I've been dragged hardly fills me with any joy, though I suppose I should be pleased with myself that I'm to speak to Lisabet herself and not one of her frown-down-my-nose-at-you personal assistants.

We stop at the door right at the end of the passage, and the man on my left raps a quick tattoo on the wood.

A muffled "Enter" follows, and we obey.

Lisabet's office is the epitome of comfort. Much to my surprise, the walls are covered floor to ceiling with books, and a veritable forest of potted plants crowds the large double doors that open onto a balcony. Her desk is a solid mahogany thing that takes pride of place in the left-hand corner, and she peers at us from over tinted halfmoon glasses as we come to a halt before her.

"So, this is the intruder," she muses, seemingly to herself.

I estimate Lisabet to be somewhere in her mid-fifties, her grey hair a fright about a round face I would have described as friendly if it weren't for the fact that she's made dire threats related to my personal sovereignty and Alessandra's purity.

"Gave Selene quite the start, Leon tells me," says the henchman on my right.

"And yet Selene is the one who caught him." Lisabet's smile is anything but pleasant, and she reaches for a long-stemmed pipe resting on its holder on her desk. She regards me as one would something soft and unpleasant that belongs in a nightsoil bucket.

If I didn't hurt all over, I'd be squirming. Those dark, kohl-rimmed eyes don't miss a thing.

"You're the only get off Bella de Lyse, aren't you?" she asks as she puffs.

I nod miserably.

"You know, she used to work for me, don't you?"

Really? I can't imagine my mother ever putting up with this horrible woman's nonsense.

Lisabet gives a dry chuckle. "You don't believe me, boy, but it's true. Your mother was quite the little rebel, I'll have you know. Unfortunately, our association...did not work out. But The House of Red Lions has been more to her taste." Her lips curl slightly then she draws on the pipe a little harder this time so that the weed in the bowl crackles. "And now… You. What on earth shall we do with you?"

"Let her go." My words come out as a cracked whisper. "You can keep me. Do anything with me. Just let her go."

"You?" Now she cackles. "You're too old and gangly to work among my catamites, and we certainly don't have employment opportunities for *burglars*."

The henchman on my right sniggers quietly and tightens his grip on my arm. I'm almost grateful, because I don't know whether I can stand on my own.

"But now what I'd really like to know, did Victor put you up to this, or did you truly develop noble aspirations of rescuing a damsel in distress?" Lisabet leans forward, and I swear little embers flash in her eyes.

"I'm here for my woman," I state with as much authority as I can muster. Which isn't much, because facing Lisabet is like facing a giant cat when you're the mouse. Any moment she'll swipe and end me. Or pack me away in one of those coffins in her basement. A shudder courses down my spine, and I'm sure my abject terror shows on my face, despite my best attempts to appear resolute.

"Tsk. So brave and foolhardy. So stupid. Now that I get a proper look at you, I have my doubts that we'll even get our weight in silver back from selling you to the Colonies. What do you think, Stefan?" She turns her gaze the man on my left.

"Ma'am, some silver is better than none. He has proved to be quite acrobatic. Perhaps he'll be of use to the excavations in the Deiran Necropolis? He entered through one of our air shafts, after all." Grudging respect laces his words.

"Did he now?" She regards me with renewed interest. "Well, then we may be able to get even more silver for his contract, don't you think?"

The Deiran Necropolis? That's not just across the Hierathic Ocean, that's all the way down to South Veronia, to the desert highlands. No indentured have ever returned from there. Alive, that is. Choking fear crawls up from my bowels and shakes me by the throat.

"Why you looking so grim, lad? Would you rather we sell your contract to the cotton plantations in Luca? Or to the silk farmers in Geme?"

I shake my head vigorously. None of this pleases me.

"Well, then what must we do with you? You do realise that we can't let you go now."

"M-my family. They know about—" Oh goodness. Does this woman even know about Alessandra? Who she really is? If not, this may well move even more pieces into the war that is brewing.

The woman tosses back her head and laughs. "Do you honestly think your family is going to retrieve one little pawn like you? And who do you think will ferry them across the waters? All the gondola men here are in my employ, and by default to my patron, who, when I last checked, was not exactly on speaking terms with yours. They know better than to start a war over one little piece like you. Your days on the board are over."

"At least let my woman go," I choke out.

"Your fine little woman. Ah. Let me think about that." Lisabet gazes skywards.

"She didn't ask for any of this."

"Oh, but I think she has. By default. Besides, even for a mixed-blood she's pretty enough. Almost good enough to look noble born but she swears and bites like a gutter rat. I think she'll do very well here."

*She doesn't know...*

I sag in my captors' hold. Lisabet has absolutely no idea she holds an heir of one of the Sun princes. I don't know whether I should be grateful. Even now the Diamas come to pluck her from this dank islet. I only hope I live long enough to apologise to Alessandra for this terrible ordeal I've subjected her to.

"Don't be sad, boy. You're both more valuable alive than dead."

To her goons, she says. "Take him and keep him in the third chamber where the novices are. Make sure he's well bound. We don't want him to damage himself or draw undue attention to his whereabouts."

And just like that I'm dismissed – mere goods to be traded. My worth measured in silver.

My vision blurs with helpless tears, but I know better than to scream and yell. No one here is going to help me. And if what Lisabet has said holds any truth, I'm not even certain my family will pull through for me, even if it means preventing an incident that will stir the Ardent's figurative muddy waters into a torrent.

Small mercies, this time the room they dump me in is an actual room and not a glorified storage cabinet. After they make sure that my bonds are tight – even my feet are bound together – and that the makeshift gag they ram into mouth won't come loose, they leave me, and the door shuts with a horrible finality. The fact that they don't bother to lock it feels like a final slap through the face.

Human trafficking. I should have put two and two together far sooner. Really, the clues were all there in that love letter Lisabet's people left in my tenement. The House of Magnolias has always been a front. For all I know, Alessandra will share a similar fate to mine if she doesn't end up serving on her back here. Although what Lisabet is doing is not strictly speaking illegal – if someone owes substantial debts, their debtors are well within their rights to sell their contract as an indentured worker – an all-out shit storm will make landfall if word gets out that a Sun heir has been whored out like a common slattern. There's no telling how many heads will roll. As in the literal sense. I suppose, in a way, my actions may well lead to social reform for the better... But of course, I may not be around to see any of this happen.

Bleak despair washes through me as I lie there. My captors weren't exactly careful about dropping me on the cot pressed against the one wall. My legs are dangling off the end, and I have to wriggle worm-like to position myself better. Not that the cot is at all comfortable. How long are they going to keep me here? What if I need to take care of necessities? At the mere thought of taking a slash, my bladder contracts in a way that tells me I haven't gone in far too long. The only thing worse than lying here on my own, waiting for them to decide what to do with me is me lying here, doing exactly that, in a pool of my own urine.

So tight are my bonds I can no longer feel my extremities, and wave after wave of panic washes through me when I realise I'm unable to move. I'm most certainly not a candidate for rough bedroom play. That ridiculous thought is so incongruous I choke back a laugh that's almost a sob, but then the mere fact that a revolting rag is half stuffed down my throat makes me gag. Add to that that one of my nostrils is blocked, it's difficult to breathe, and the panic is back. What if my remaining nostril clogs up? I'll suffocate! My lungs are bellows expanding and contracting in ever-wheezier heaves.

I hate the little whimpers that creep up past my lips, but I can't help myself as I squirm like bait on the end of a hook until I fall to the floor. The impact drives the air from my lungs, and for an eternity of gargling and choking, I'm convinced that I'm dying.

That's when the door to my prison opens and someone slips in.

I still immediately. Footsteps thump past outside in the passage, two men talking in low, measured tones.

That's when I look up to see who has entered.

Alessandra, her back pressed to the door as she stares down at me. In the time that she's been here, she's been garbed in a tight-fitting plum corset with matching skirts that are shorter at the front to reveal her knees, and slim, calf-high boots that show off her shapely legs. She's been primped and painted so that she is scarcely recognisable, her startling hazel eyes heavily outlined with kohl and shaded with malachite. Her hair, however, gleams, loose and wild, and its rich mahogany hue is unmistakeable. In her right hand she clutches a basket-hilt rapier. Its point is sticky-red with someone's blood.

I frown. "Anglahghghgghaarrghh," is unfortunately all I can say.

A moment passes as we regard each other in shocked silence then she kneels quickly before me and tugs at the gag so that it comes loose.

"Ben? What on earth are you doing here?"

"I came to rescue you," I croak.

To this she gives a small, bright peal of laughter. "Then we must hurry, because it's only a matter of time before they notice that I've managed to get out of my room." She starts working on the bindings on my hands.

"How..."

"No one's laid a hand on me, yet," she says as she tugs. "They've really gone and made these knots tight. Any longer and you'd suffer damage."

Another tug, and my hands flop loose. She helps me sit upright, but while the blood is rushing back to my extremities with an astonishingly painful prickle of pins and needles, I'm all but useless.

"What did you do to yourself? You look like you've been torn at by wild animals."

"In a manner of speaking I have." I offer her a crooked grin. She smells so clean, so sweet, like musk roses and jasmine.

"And you came here for me?" Her eyebrows arch in a perfect poise of astonishment.

I nod, even if the gesture makes my head swim. "It's my fault you're here."

"Well, all things considered, it's either here or having my fingers chopped off by an overzealous thug, and to be honest I'd sooner be here than there. But honestly, Ben." She tuts, shakes her head. "You shouldn't have." She finishes with the bindings on my feet then rises.

"But..."

"Do I look as if I need rescuing?"

"But..." My mind is sluggish, incapable of turning over the facts my senses are feeding it.

"If anything, you're the one who needs a hand. You're just incredibly lucky that I chose this particular room to hide in when I heard those idiots clomping down the passage." She helps me up, and to my eternal mortification, I'm the one who has to lean on her. "Those footpads should be gone by now. We have precious little time."

Alessandra opens the door a crack and peers out, then we're off, hurrying in the opposite direction.

"There's a central passage," I murmur.

"I know. Where do you think I'm going?"

I shut up and concentrate on putting each foot before the other, because my legs are wobblier than those of a drunkard who's had a few shots of firetongue too many.

"Now, I swear the door was around here somewhere."

She lets go of me, and I clutch at the wall while she feels at the edges of what looks like a painting. A latch clicks.

"Hah!"

Before I have the chance to protest at the rough treatment, she shoves me in ahead of her and shuts the door behind us. And not a moment too soon, because a man starts shouting in the distance. Whether they've seen us vanish into the stairwell is anyone's guess, but we're not going to linger to find out.

"Let me go first," Alessandra says. "And put your hand on my shoulder for support. You look like you're about to keel over."

I nod sickly then wish I hadn't, because a wave of nausea makes me gulp back air.

"And for the Gods' and Saints' sakes both, if you're going to vomit, don't do it on me."

"I'll try," I say in a small voice.

She gets a firm grip on my left upper arm and then we start our descent. We're not even two flights down when a door opens above us.

"They're here!" a man shouts. "Get Bruno to go round the other side."

"Fuck," Alessandra says.

I blanch. Not that I've never heard a woman swear. It's just that that one little word is so unexpected from her perfect lips.

"What now?" I hate how my voice croaks on that last syllable. The air inside this spiralling staircase is too close, too laden with the slow reek of damp.

"We keep going," she says then tugs.

"There's a door in one of the lower storerooms," I tell her. "It leads outside, and I don't think they'll expect us to go that route."

She pauses, looks over her shoulder. "You sure about that?"

"You planning on fighting your way out of here armed only with a rapier?"

Alessandra gives a small cough of laughter. "You may have a point. Fine. Tell me where to go."

Even as she finishes the last words, a door opens in the stairwell a floor above us, and one of Lisabet's thugs comes thundering down with a triumphant cry. The man all but leaps down at us, but Alessandra is faster. I hardly have a moment to cry out when she lunges over me, and the man impales himself on the rapier's business end. Startlement is writ over his features as he grasps his predicament – that a woman should be his death is inconceivable. He clutches feebly at the blade before she rips it from his chest. Hells, even I didn't expect it.

The man drops, and we continue on our headlong flight down the stairs.

"Where did you learn to fight?" I ask.

"Did you really think I spent all my time learning to embroider and play lute?" she shoots back.

Then we're at the door. Or at least I think it's the door we need. My vision is swimming, and my nausea is back in full force, but I daren't let her down now.

Alessandra has hardly broken a sweat, and she waits while I listen at the door. I can't hear anything beyond, but there's a commotion upstairs. The music has stopped, and people are shouting.

"We don't have all night." Alessandra pushes open the door, and we enter the passage. It's deserted. For now.

To my eternal shame, it's me she's supporting as we make our way back to the storerooms, according to my directions. By now it's clear that wholesale armed conflict has broken out upstairs.

"What's going on?" she asks with a meaningful glance to the ceiling.

"I don't know, but I think..." I wet my lips. "My family might have arrived. I hope."

"You *hope*. That's hardly reassuring."

We round a corner, and all seems fine until footsteps rush up behind us. As one, Alessandra and I twist to face the two men who slow to a stroll the moment they register Alessandra's drawn blade.

"I wouldn't come any closer," I warn, though my voice is shaky. "She knows how to use a sword."

"Thanks," she mutters under her breath even as she pushes me behind her. Under ordinary circumstances, I'd bristle at such treatment, but considering that I'm unarmed and unsteady, her apparent chivalry is welcome. Besides, I've never much been one for duels.

The larger of the two men laughs and draws his blade. It's a short, ugly thing, meant for sticking someone in close quarters. The second one is armed with a rapier. Dismay blooms in my stomach. Two of them at the same time? Just how good is she?

While short sword moves to our left, rapier man comes right at us. Alessandra parries elegantly, and dances around both even as big guy tries to get in a stab. Either he's focused on her or he's completely discounted me, which is fine. Wobbly as I am, I dart in and grab the dirk from its sheath at his belt, but I'm not fast enough to move out of the way as he knocks me hard across the ear with an elbow.

Stars fill my vision, and I connect intimately with the wall before I sag to the ground, but I hold onto that blade. Any advantage now is preferable. A boot connects with my ribs and drives all the air from my lungs, and for a moment all I can do is curl into a foetal ball. Metal clashes on metal, as if from a great distance, but then a man cries out. The next blow I expect doesn't land, and although my world is obscured by a haze of agony,

I uncurl and roll onto my haunches in time to see the man with the short sword press Alessandra against the wall. The rapier man is groaning on the ground about five paces from me.

"I should cut you for this, bitch," the short sword man grates into Alessandra's face. Her rapier lies discarded on the ground, and he has such a firm hold on her throat with one hand her feet are raised from the ground. With his left hand he's crushing her right against the wall.

"Oh no you don't," I mutter as I lunge.

Sure, I've been in knife fights – enough to know where and when to stab a man. He has his back to me and that dirk of his is nice and sharp. A blade to the kidney is invariably fatal, and the results are instantaneous. He cries out and drops, and I lurch forward to catch Alessandra before she falls. I don't know who holds up the other, because we slide down the wall in a sweaty, mucky heap of fabric, our faces close enough for a lovers' kiss.

Her eyes are huge, and she's gasping for air, but appears otherwise unharmed.

"This is—"

"Awkward. Now, let's keep going." With a cough, she rises and pulls me up with her. Alessandra pauses long enough to grab her rapier, and then we're off down the passage.

I have a bad moment when I'm confused about where we need to be, but then we find the right door, and she helps me unstick the bar. Thanks all the Gods I still have my trusty little back-up pick, but my hands are trembling so violently I drop my tools twice before I can continue questing for the right order in the tumblers.

All the while, Alessandra keeps watch, and the yells and clashing of metal on metal grow louder.

"Hurry up, will you," she says.

"Do you want to do this?" I glare at her. "This isn't something that should be rushed."

"Any longer and they'll find us here. Either your lot or our esteemed host's, and I get the feeling neither will have our best interests at heart. The Diamas serve with the Cordos. I might be a Sun princess but I'm not stupid."

"All right, all right," I mutter.

It's one thing to pick locks when you've got only yourself to disappoint. It's quite another thing with an audience. I don't do audiences, and it's almost impossible to pretend that the woman I love is not breathing over my shoulder while I gamely attempt to unlock a door. My fingers are slick, and I can't quite keep the grip on my tools, but then the tumblers roll into place, the mechanism clicks, and we shove the door open.

And not a moment too soon. Even as we shut the door, a knot of men pelts past, calling out to each other. I'm not quite sure what they're saying, because the sounds echo strangely, but it's just the two of us here, now. Alone.

I sag against the door. "Buggering hell."

Alessandra's already pacing to the door leading to outside that's across the room from us. She peers out of the little window then spins about and marches straight back to me. "C'mon, Ben. Don't waste time."

"Give me a moment. Please." I stow my tools back in my boot then rise, resting with my hands on my knees while I catch my breath.

Alessandra's restless, a predator in a too-small cage, and out of the corner of my eye, I'm aware of how she pokes about until she picks up an object. It's my tool pouch.

"You've found my picks," I say. Surely this is a turn in

my fortune. A fierce joy surges through me.

Alessandra peeks inside then passes me the pouch. The thong is broken, so I can't hang it around my neck, but I stick it into the pocket of my breeches.

She shakes her head, her smile in the low light wry. "I can't believe everything that's happened in the past few hours. I keep reading about high adventure and derring-do, but I never once imagined I'd find myself in the thick of it."

I gape at her. "You were in danger of losing your fingers or...worse."

"But it never happened, did it?"

"Angelo Cordo wouldn't have been as soft as the men of Lisabet's house of dubious pleasures," I point out.

"Are you so sure about that?"

I forget. She's killed two men today and hasn't so much as blinked. When I killed my first man at the not-so-tender age of thirteen, I'd vomited. She doesn't even seem perturbed. Unease stirs, and I shake my head. "Well. Let's go. I'll get you back to your father...or your fiancé."

"My father. I think we've established that this charade has gone on long enough, don't you think?"

"Very well." I bow then make my way to the door leading outside. I can't see much beyond the dirty glass, and I can only pray no one's lurking outside.

While the lock is rusty, I work it quick enough, and we both shove to get it open when it won't at first budge. The shouting is much louder now, accompanied by the crash of broken glass and women shrieking. That's when it hits me, and I turn to Alessandra.

"Uh, how good are you with swimming?"

A small frown mars her forehead. "If it has to be done, it has to be done. I'm not staying here a moment longer."

"Wait here," I tell her and creep out, only to realise

that she's following close on my heels.

Riotous growth overhangs most of this area – a dense canopy of flowering moonshine vine with its characteristic sprays of heart-shaped leaves, I guess to hide this exit from the casual eye. The vegetation serves us well now.

We freeze when two men rush along the pathway just ahead, but we can't see past the moonshine vine to establish who they are. At any rate, I can't trust my own family on this task I must now fulfil, and even if I succeed, I'll no doubt be rewarded with a dip in Dog's Row quarry with chains wrapped round me to ensure I stay down.

Then we're off, and I lead Alessandra down the terraces until we reach the water's edge, where several gondolas bob. The lone figure keeping watch spots us immediately.

Alessandra steps forward, her rapier at the ready, her entire posture warning that she's about to do something rash.

"Don't!" I say. "It's Cael." As if that would explain everything.

She turns to me. "This is your friend?"

Cael shakes his head as if he can't quite believe his eyes. "Ben, Ben, Ben, what have you done now?"

"We're escaping," I tell him. "And you're going to give us one of those gondolas."

"Most assuredly not. We're going to wait here until the others realise she's not upstairs, and then we're all going to leave and set this to rights. The Cordos need to be placated."

"I'm not going to the Cordos." Alessandra steps forward.

"I must warn you, she's killed two of Lisabet's thugs already. She knows how to use that thing," I say, then to Alessandra, I add, "Please don't hurt him. He's my only friend."

Cael holds up his hands. "Peace, please. We don't need to shed any more blood than has already been spilled."

I don't even want to consider the ramifications of tonight's unplanned sortie. It's going to take weeks to smooth over the damage. That's if I'm even here or alive to bear witness.

"And I am not some prize to be squabbled over by Shadow princes with half-baked notions about the worth of fingers. Here's what we're going to do." She points that rapier at Cael so that it pauses a hand's breadth from his chest. "I'm taking you hostage. That way you can claim that it was all Ben's doing, and you're going to row back to where we need to be. Now."

Cael snorts laughter and looks over Alessandra's shoulder to me. "What? Are you so addled that you're taking orders from a mere slip of a—"

He doesn't get a chance to finish because she lunges and pushes him into the water. The mud is slippery, and he loses his footing immediately.

"Get in the boat, Ben," she orders me. "And start pushing that pole before I start making holes in your idiot friend here while he flounders about like a beached sea serpent."

Cael has stopped splashing and spluttering, because the needle-thin point of the rapier is touching the tip of his nose. He's staring at it with a cross-eyed look of complete horror.

I select one of the smaller gondolas and grab the pole. Alessandra waits until the last minute then steps up onto the boat, and we're off, sliding across the water. We must make a right pair – Alessandra dressed like a lady of dubious virtue and me looking like I've been attacked by a wild animal. But we're free, and the sounds of fighting die down as we put distance between ourselves and The House of Magnolias.

Once we're in the quieter, weed-choked channels where the merchants have their homes, she speaks. "You know, all of this could have been avoided if you'd just let me wait nearby until the Cordos were done and then taken me to my father."

"Why did you come with me then?"

Her teeth flash in a small smile. "I was curious. I mean, here's this young man who's spent nearly every hour I've been at the library holding vigil. You've never once approached, just sat there, pretending so hard that you're not staring."

"You could have sent your guardsmen to sort me out, chase me off. Why didn't you?"

Alessandra gives a small shrug. "I was telling myself a story, that you were really a Sun prince fallen into the Shadow. Or you were a young Shadow prince on the up and up, and you'd eventually do something rash and romantic by declaring your love for me with a bunch of flowers or a kitten.

"But no. Day in and day out for the last six months, you're there. And I like your face, you're not pretty and you're not handsome, but there's something compelling about your features that I enjoyed pretending to not look at."

My heart does somersaults. "I-is this your way of saying that you like me?"

"Maybe. I must admit the timing of your visit was a little too convenient. I thought perhaps it was a ruse, that you were in cahoots with the Cordos. But you genuinely looked like you were fearing for my life. And if I am entirely honest… That's kind of sweet."

"And then I needed rescuing," I mumble.

"So?" She plays idly with a ringlet of hair that has

escaped its fastenings. "Lady Fortune has a strange way of smiling sometimes. If you had not been there to overhear the Cordos' plans, if Lisabet had not insisted on collecting her debt, if I had not stumbled into that room to escape the thugs, we wouldn't be sitting here, now."

"It does all seem rather...like destiny."

"But you can't woo me, Ben. I hope you understand that, don't you?"

My throat closes up, and I nod.

"My wedding is in two weeks, and I'm sure my fiancé will be anxious to move the date forward now thanks to the Cordos."

"But you don't love him, do you?"

"He's not a cruel man. I could have done worse."

"Come away with me," I say. "We can board one of the colony ships. There's one that's just docked."

"And break our backs working on someone else's plantation?"

"But you don't love him."

"Love is not important in my world. The mask we present to others is. What are you going to do?"

"I... I will have to face up to what I've done." I heave out a sigh. My wild hopes have evaporated. If she stays, then so must I, though I can't tell her that.

"You're a good man, Ben. Far better than the others I've met. Keep a hold of that goodness. You're going to need it."

Surely, there has to be a way for us to make things work, but we enter a busy waterway where dozens of barges crowd each other, and we have to keep watch in case we are marked... I have no desire to be crushed between two of those wallowing vessels. And then we're in the eastern isles, hushing among the reeds, and we don't have much time anymore.

The sky is turning grey, and I can assess how badly bruised and hurt I am. So many scrapes and lacerations, and it's difficult for me to pinpoint the pain exactly, because it's spread throughout my body. My clothing is completely ruined, and I don't have any spare. I am no better than a beggar, and I have even fewer prospects considering that my family will no doubt punish me, and do so severely.

Thing is, even though Alessandra is dressed so gaudily, she nonetheless still exudes elegance, from the arch of her lovely neck to her watchfulness. Her eyes miss nothing. She keeps that rapier flat on her lap, her right hand curled around the handle, as if at any moment now she'll spring into action. If only I had my artist's materials at my disposal, so that I may make a charcoal sketch to capture the essence of her loveliness, and perhaps even suggest the danger lying beneath such a fair veneer.

Our moment of stillness is broken as cormorants take wing, and an ibis honks like a broken wind instrument from a lazy willow across the waterway. Here, passing between the homes of the Sun princes and their scions, it is easy to believe that we exist in a world separate from the blood and terror from scant hours earlier.

"Will you be all right?" I ask as we near her family's private jetty with its little ornate boathouse. "Should I perhaps walk you a small way?"

For a heartbeat it looks as if she'll laugh at my offer of assistance, but then she nods. "I'd like that."

I get out of the gondola and make it fast against its mooring, then offer her my arm as though I were an impeccably attired gentleman. This entire scene is like something out of one of the absurdist plays Cael and I sometimes go watch.

Her touch is light as she places her left hand on my arm – more for show than anything else – because she's quite capable of stepping out of the boat and onto solid ground unaided. Also, she's not relinquished her grip on the rapier, which she holds point down as I let her slip her left arm into the crook of my right.

"Imagine that we are strolling along the Promenade," I tell her. "The sun is setting – it is the Day of Stars, and we can hear the cantor at the Shrine of Mermaids offer up his early evening psalms."

Alessandra gives a soft snort. "Who'd have thought. You have the heart and tongue of a poet."

We stroll quietly through the thicket, along the path leading towards the palace. Small frogs pipe among the masses of ferns, and in the distance splashes the musical tinkle of a water feature.

I pause, turn to face her. "I'm sorry it has come to this."

A small frown creases her brow. "Really now, Ben. Don't apologise. Not everyone's cut out to be a hero. And you're a rotten foot soldier, too." But she smiles and snakes up her hand to pull me down for a kiss.

# EPILOGUE

In the days and nights that follow, I replay that last scene with Alessandra in a thousand ways. The softness of her lips, the scent of her, despite the overwhelming perfumes Lisabet's people foisted on her. The way topaz motes in her hazel eyes gleam. Oh, how I kiss those lips in my dreams. Never before has a parting brought such sweet sorrow.

I watched that fateful morning, screened by a thick stand of ornamental bamboo, as she walked up the footpath. She did not look back.

Cael says I'm lucky Victor hasn't sold me to the Colonies for a sum that won't even make a dent in the bother I caused with the whole "princess job debacle" as the incident involving Alessandra has now become known. But I don't see Cael much these days, as I've been demoted. No one ever leaves the family, unless it's feet first out the door. So, while I've not been cast off or am currently sleeping on the river's silty bed, I'm no longer collecting our dues and roughing up anyone who crosses us.

Instead, for the past two months, I've been a lookout and a glorified errand boy. The only blessings I see in this are that I now live in the room under the stairs in Cael's tenement, where people can't break in to steal my things. Also, Lisabet has mysteriously written off my debt. Cael says the Saints must be watching out for me, after all. I have my suspicions about who might have had my debt cleared, but I won't voice them.

I haven't been back to the library gardens since that night. I can't bear to.

And the wedding took place two weeks ago. All of the bells of Ardent rang for an hour during noon. Whatever twisted, weird moment she and I shared that one night, it's over. And I'm lucky to be alive. It's as Alessandra's said: I'm not a hero.

But I have started writing. Mostly short stories about a guardsman who gets caught up in the criminal underworld. And poems. Terrible, lovelorn poems. Figure I may as well write what I know. Maybe I can get one of the local publishers to make a serial out of my stories. Cael says so long as we can't recognise any real persons, and I publish under a nom de plume, Victor won't want to cut off my fingers.

I told him I'll write with my toes if I have to.

I read a piece in one of the literary journals I picked up at the second-hand bookstore, that says how each of us has one great disappointment in our lives that defines us, that makes us taste the fleeting sweetness of life and cherish it for the fact that it's gone. And that we tasted it at all. There's a word for it. Ephem— Or something. Doesn't matter. I'm not a great poet, as much as I harbour the pretentions. I write what I feel, what burns in me. I make worlds that are not the world where I am now. Where I'm someone who matters, who changes things for the better.

Cael says I'm still young, that we'll figure things out. And Victor can't stay pissed off with me forever, because like it or not, we did stop a war from happening—even if it was my fault things got so bad in the first place. Many more people would have died.

I wish this made me feel better.

\*

Autumn comes slowly to the Ardent delta. At first there's a slight nip in the air, and in the mornings thin mist curls in lazy swirls on the river. Fine clouds of midges dance in the late-afternoon sun, and sometimes fish lip at the surface to catch them. The flame trees' leaves turn from green to yellow, and then brilliant red, and it is as if the city is on fire for the brief days before the first winds blow down from the north, bringing with it the chill of slow ice on winter's breath.

It's late, and I'm on my own – a rare night off – and I've spent most of it at The Tin Teacup listening to the poets read. I've been plucking up the courage to read my poems up on the stage, but tonight is not the night. The pages are crumpled inside my jacket's left pocket. All good folks are asleep and dreaming at this hour, but I'm not good folks nor do I wish to dream, for of late my sleep has been plagued by one unfortunate scenario after the other, how things could have turned out different. Better. Or often worse.

I'm careful. This isn't Diama territory. I'm dangerously close to a no-man's land shared by numerous Shadow princes – mainly because no one can ever make up their bleeding minds about who should be in control here. Which also means that stuff that goes down in these parts tends to be ignored for fear of sparking greater conflict.

As I turn down a lane that will take me to the bridge to the next isle that I realise I'm not alone. The clever thing to do is to keep walking, make like I'm not bothered, but I slide my knife from its sheath. Except I'm expecting someone behind me, so when my stalker leaps out before me, from a stack of old crates, I'm caught wrong footed.

They're smaller than me, wreathed in a dark cloak, and an icy lick of a blade at my throat warns me not to move. But I look down, and in the gloom those hazel eyes wink back at me, followed by a smile as wicked as her blade.

"You really are shit at your job," says Alessandra.

"I'm off duty tonight." I relax a little. Cael will have my fruit for breakfast if he hears about me being taken by surprise. I should know better by now.

"It's almost like you were inviting someone to slit your throat."

"Ah, but you won't, and I think we've both established that you are far more canny than the average foot soldier."

Alessandra gives a soft snort. "Admittedly, you were difficult to find. You haven't been to the library garden of late."

"And you, a married woman. Surely you would be kept busy playing house with your new man?"

It's the wrong thing to say, for she shoves me away from her and pulls her cloak around her. Her teeth flash small and white in the gloom. "I never said I was marrying for love. Or excitement."

"And yet here you are, stalking the streets like an alley cat. It's hardly becoming of a married woman expected to produce heirs and attend tea parties." I can't prevent my bitterness from bleeding through. This is not how I imagined our reunion. I did not want to ruin that one perfect kiss at dawn.

"And how would you know how women keep themselves, married or not?"

I shrug, for obviously I know nothing.

Her laugh is ragged. "Do you know what a beard is?"

I goggle at her. "What are you getting at?" I'm genuinely confused. She's not talking about real facial hair, is she?

"Oh, my dear sweet man, you really can be naïve." She slips her arm into mine, and I'm forced to stumble after her.

"The night is but a pup, Ben, and this is not a tawdry romance, where everything ties up neatly with happily-ever-afters and baby's blankets. Anything can happen."

"Um, I know a diner," I offer. "They only open at midnight. Unfortunately, there's only one item on—"

She halts and puts a finger on my lips. "Shhh. No apologies. Promise me that. Whatever happens in the shadows is ours. Let the sun take care of its own sorrows."

Alessandra Francesca Luciente. She is the most beautiful woman in all of Ardent, and she knows my name.

# ABOUT THE AUTHOR

Nerine Dorman is a South African author and editor of science fiction and fantasy currently living in Cape Town. Her novel *Sing down the Stars* won Gold for the Sanlam Prize for Youth Literature in 2019, and her YA fantasy novel *Dragon Forged* was a finalist in 2017. Her short story "On the Other Side of the Sea" (Omenana, 2017) was shortlisted for a 2018 Nommo award, and her novella *The Firebird* won a Nommo for "Best Novella" during 2019. She is the curator of the South African Horrorfest Bloody Parchment event and short story competition and is a founding member of the SFF authors' co-operative Skolion, which has assisted authors such as Masha du Toit, Suzanne van Rooyen, Cristy Zinn, and Cat Hellisen, among others, in their publishing endeavours.

*See www.nerinedorman.blogspot.com*

# OTHER BOOKS BY NERINE DORMAN

**Books of Khepera**
*Khepera Rising* (#1)
*Khepera Redeemed* (#2)

**Those Who Return**
*Inkarna* (#1)
*Thanatos* (#2)

*Camdeboo Nights*

**The Gatekeeper Cycle**
*The Guardian's Wyrd* (#1)

*Dawn's Bright Talons*

**The Blackfeather Chronicles**
Raven Kin (#1)

*Lost Children* (short story anthology)

*In Southern Darkness* (two novellas)

*The Firebird* (novella)

*The Company of Birds*

*Sing down the Stars*

*Aetheria* (short story)

*Dragon Forged* (novella)